W9-BZW-985

TRANSFERRAL

3 3133 02819 5241

KATE BLAIR

TRANSFERRAL

Central Rappahannock Regional Library
1201 Caroline Street
Fredericksburg, VA 22401

YA
Bla
c. 2

Copyright © 2015 Kate Blair
This edition © 2015 Dancing Cat Books, an imprint of Cormorant Books Inc.
First published in the United States in 2016
This is a first edition.

No part of this publication may be reproduced, stored in a retrieval system
or transmitted, in any form or by any means, without the prior written consent
of the publisher or a licence from The Canadian Copyright Licensing Agency
(Access Copyright). For an Access Copyright licence,
visit www.accesscopyright.ca or call toll free 1.800.893.5777.

 Canada Council   Conseil des Arts   ONTARIO ARTS COUNCIL
for the Arts   du Canada   CONSEIL DES ARTS DE L'ONTARIO
                                       an Ontario government agency
                                       un organisme du gouvernement de l'Ontario

Canadian   Patrimoine    Canada
Heritage   canadien

The publisher gratefully acknowledges the support of the Canada Council for the Arts
and the Ontario Arts Council for its publishing program. We acknowledge the
financial support of the Government of Canada through the Canada Book Fund (CBF)
for our publishing activities, and the Government of Ontario through the
Ontario Media Development Corporation, an agency of the Ontario Ministry
of Culture, and the Ontario Book Publishing Tax Credit Program.

LIBRARY AND ARCHIVES CANADA CATALOGUING IN PUBLICATION

Blair, Kate, author
Transferral / Kate Blair.

Issued in print and electronic formats.
ISBN 978-1-77086-454-2 (paperback). — ISBN 978-1-77086-455-9 (html)

1. Title.

PS8603.L3153T73 2015   JC813'.6   C2015-905378-1
                                        C2015-905379-X

United States Library of Congress Control Number: 2015949543

Cover photograph and design: angeljohnguerra.com
Interior text design: Tannice Goddard, bookstopress.com
Printer: Friesens

Printed and bound in Canada.
Manufactured by Friesens in Altona, Manitoba, Canada in August, 2015.

MIX
Paper from
responsible sources
FSC
www.fsc.org   FSC® C016245

This book is printed on 100% post-consumer waste recycled paper.

DANCING CAT BOOKS
AN IMPRINT OF CORMORANT BOOKS INC.
10 ST. MARY STREET, SUITE 615, TORONTO, ONTARIO, M4Y 1P9
www.dancingcatbooks.com
www.cormorantbooks.com

To my favorite soon-to-be teens

Olivia Boulton and Danielle Clayton

CHAPTER ONE

PENTHOUSE FLAT,
BANKSIDE, LONDON
*TWENTY-FOUR DAYS LEFT
UNTIL THE ELECTION*

THE KITCHEN IS CROWDED, as usual. I swallow a cough as I enter. I don't want to disgust them.

Dad is half-hidden behind a newspaper with his picture on the front. He spots me and folds it before I can read the headline. That can't be good.

Alison, Dad's executive assistant, sits across the breakfast bar. She looks me up and down, apparently surprised to see me in my pajamas. But this is my home. What does she expect?

"How's the throat today?" Dad asks.

"Worse." I touch my neck gingerly. The glands on either side of my windpipe are swollen and sore. "My head hurts too."

Dad comes over, places a sympathetic hand on my shoulder.

Piers, Dad's campaign manager, turns his body away, not looking up from his laptop.

"Have we got time to drop Talia off at the hospital for a Transfer?" Dad asks.

Alison pulls out her phone and jabs at it. Her hair falls over her face, perfect as usual, but she's wearing the same suit I saw her in yesterday. Didn't she go home last night? Did she spend it with Piers? Doubtful. A volunteer back at campaign HQ?

"Sorry. We have to be at Victoria Library at 9 a.m. To hand out literacy awards." She smiles at Dad as she says it, as though handing out literacy awards is tantamount to climbing Everest.

"And I need to brief you before then," Piers says. "A volunteer can take her to St. Barts."

Dad runs his fingers through his graying beard. "Piers, you said when we launched the campaign that we'd make time for Talia."

"And we do. Just not this morning."

"You can brief me in the car. St. Barts is a quick detour en route to Victoria."

Piers shakes his head. "She's probably contagious. We don't have time in the schedule for you to get the Transfer. You should step away from her."

"I'm standing right here," I say.

"That's the problem," Piers says. "If Malcolm gets it from you, and can't get it transferred right away, he might get caught on camera coughing or wiping his nose. He'd look like a criminal."

"We can use hand sanitizer and masks," Dad says. "Talia, can you be ready in five minutes?"

"No problem." I run upstairs before Piers can argue, glad of the opportunity to spend some time with Dad, even if it's just a car ride.

It takes me less than five minutes to put on a pencil skirt, a lambs-wool top, and a dash of makeup, but by the time I'm back downstairs, Dad's waiting in the doorway of our flat. Piers is holding the lift open with his walking stick. I grab my jacket, shrugging it on and buttoning it up as the lift doors close and we descend.

I sniff and the others move away from me. I don't blame them. The sound grosses me out too. But Dad smiles at me, and I appreciate him making the effort.

The doorman nods at us as we step out together, into the hissing bluster of a spring day.

The wind throws my long hair in my face. I try to smooth it down, to keep it from exposing the scar that runs across my scalp. The driver waits with the limo at the curb, holding the door open. Alison gives me a mask as I get in. It's a big car, with an L-shaped seat. I pull the mask over my face as I head for the corner.

Dad slides his tall frame across the back seat next to me. Piers puts his cane in the car ahead of him, climbs in, and sits on the other side, at right angles to us and as far away as he can get. Alison jumps in last, next to Dad.

The London traffic is relatively light, and I stare at the muddy Thames as we cross Southwark Bridge, my head thumping along with my pulse. I can't wait to get this disease transferred. Around me, the others put on their masks and pass around the hand sanitizer. I try not to be offended.

"How are the polls?" I ask, voice muffled by the mask.

Dad doesn't answer, so I sink back in my seat, seeing my visions of us living at 10 Downing Street slide out of sight. "That bad, huh?"

"There are twenty-four days until the election. Don't worry," Dad says.

Piers butts in. "Now Malcolm, about those ads." He starts talking about key messages and strong visuals. I want to focus, but my head is full of aching mist. So I tune out the discussion as London flashes by, blurring into a mass of gray.

After a while, Piers falls silent, and Alison's voice cuts my mental fog.

"Where do you think you got it, Talia?"

"What?"

"This illness. It's not like you've been hanging out with criminals."

It's a rude question, but a fair point. It's been over a year since I was last sick. Since everyone I know gets their illnesses transferred at the first symptoms, I hardly ever catch anything. People are at their most contagious when their noses are running and they're hacking up clouds of germs, and only criminals end up like that.

"That drunk man on Bridge Street last week," Piers says. "Remember? He sneezed as we were walking by."

Of course. He stank of stale beer and was ranting and swearing at passersby.

"I told you we should have crossed the road to avoid him," Piers says.

I wish I'd listened to him. My throat really hurts. We sit in silence for a minute.

"Want to interview me?" Dad says.

He's trying to cheer me up. It's a game we've been playing since he became a politician. I pretend to be a hardball interviewer. Ask questions to help Dad practise. He has real media people for this, of course, but it's still nice to be included.

"Sure." I make my hand into a loose fist and stick it in Dad's face. The invisible microphone.

"The National Law Party are well behind the Democratic Justice Party. What makes you think you can still win?"

Dad puts on his serious face. "Because we have to. Otherwise Sebastian Conway and the Democratic Justice Party will take this country straight to hell. He'll cut funding for universities, for schools, for the National Transfer Service, and invest it all in criminals."

I bring the invisible microphone back to my face. "What would you say to those who claim he's tackling inequality?"

"I'd say they were idiots," Piers mutters. But Dad keeps a straight face. Keeps on playing his role.

"Poverty isn't to blame for criminality, and it's an insult to the poor to say so. When I was a child, my parents hit tough times when my father lost his business. We were often hungry, but we never broke the law."

I'm nodding. It's hard to keep up the tough-interviewer facade. Especially with this headache. But I keep going.

"The current government still hold on to some core support, in spite of their convictions for embezzling public funds. Do you think they could win?"

Dad shakes his head. "They're corrupt. They stole from our country. You can't have criminals running the UK."

"But without those convictions, you would be the leader of a third party, with no chance in this election. Some would say it was only an accident of circumstances that you've got this far."

"It's no accident. The choice is between us, the convicts of the current government, or Sebastian Conway and his criminal-friendly Democratic Justice Party. The choice is between law and order and criminals."

"You're saying 'criminals' too much," Piers interrupts. "Vary your word usage. Thugs, convicts, lawbreakers, crooks, violent felons, killers, rapists. And Talia, you're a terrible interviewer. You go too easy on him. Practically feed him lines."

"You were great," Dad says, eyes smiling over his mask.

Piers is right, of course. But playing devil's advocate is tough when the other side is so unreasonable. There are rumors that Sebastian Conway wants to get rid of the Transfer system altogether. How can he be winning?

We turn at the entrance to St. Barts, a magnificent white building with an archway watched over by the stern gaze of Henry VIII, hands on wide hips.

"When will I see you next?" I ask Dad.

He glances at Alison, who produces her phone again. "We're having brunch with supporters in Knightsbridge at ten o'clock. If you're done in time, you can join us there. But we're leaving for Manchester right after that. We won't be back until past your bedtime."

"I'm sixteen. I don't have a bedtime."

"Sorry. No offence intended."

I raise an eyebrow.

"I'll send a car for you," Piers says. "If it's past ten it'll take you home. There's no point in coming to Knightsbridge if we're nearly done."

"I'll be done by then." It hurts a little when I speak.

In the courtyard we pull up outside the shiny glass of the new wing. Piers has called ahead and there's a security guard waiting outside for me. Dad twists to the side so I can push past him on the way out of the car. I want to give him a kiss but my mask is in the way. And I'm contagious.

I follow the guard into the lobby. His footsteps echo through the glass-and-marble space at a marching pace. I trot behind him, too ill to keep up. This sort of special treatment makes me feel weird. But it would be dangerous for the daughter of a prime ministerial candidate to wait with everyone else.

The security guard gets me checked in at reception and leads me up to an assessment room. After he leaves, I perch on the edge of the bed, stare at the antiseptic white space, and check my phone. Eight-fifty. I can easily be done by ten.

Almost immediately, the door swings open. A black guy stands in the frame. I think he might be a nurse at first, but he's too young, and wearing jeans, not scrubs. His eyes catch my attention, a startling shade of emerald.

"Hi," I say, trying not to look at his chest. His T-shirt fits him well.

"Umm." He glances around, then his green eyes meet mine. "Don't suppose you've seen a big guy around, have you? Might be acting a bit weird."

"No. I haven't. Or, well, I don't think I have. What does he look like?" I'm babbling. Why am I babbling?

"This tall." He holds a hand above his head. "Darker skin than mine. About so wide."

I nod my understanding, trying not to cough. I don't want to scare him away. His eyes widen. "You've seen him?"

"Oh, no, sorry. I meant I'll keep an eye out for him."

His shoulder slump. "Thanks."

I don't want him to go. I don't get a chance to meet guys these days.

"What should I do if I see him? Should I, um, call you or something?"

When did I become a stammering idiot?

"Nah. I'd better just keep looking."

Then he sneezes. I lean back, even though he's yards away. Try not to look disgusted. After all, I'm sick too. We're all here for the Transfer.

Before I can say anything else he ducks back out. The door slams shut, making me jump.

Well, I messed that one up. He must think I'm a total airhead. It's good I'll probably never see him again.

I exhale, kicking my feet. I keep checking my phone. Nine-oh-two … Nine-ten … Nine-eighteen … Finally, the nurse comes in. She pushes her frizzy hair behind her ears as she examines the chart she's carrying.

"Miss Hale?"

"Call me Talia."

She walks over, flipping through the chart. "Right hand please, Miss Hale."

I hold it out. She produces a needle, then pricks my finger. I'm careful not to flinch at the sting of it.

"Have you been working here long?" I cringe at the words coming out of my mouth. It must be the pounding in my head, making me dumber than usual.

"Yes," she says as she squeezes, producing a berry of blood. She smears it on a testing strip, pops that into a glass tube, seals it, and sticks on a label.

"Do you like your job?" I sound like some out-of-touch minor royal. But I'm starved for conversation with someone other than Dad and his staff.

"It's fine." She grabs a cotton ball and presses it to my finger. "Hold this," she says. "Back in a few minutes." And she's out the door before I can ask her how long "a few minutes" will be. I rest my aching head in my hands.

Nine-twenty-five. This is one of the last days Dad will be based in London. Parliament will be dissolved soon, then he's roaming all over the country on that garish campaign bus and I won't get to see him at all. Nine-twenty-nine.

I look up at the Transfer machine.

I stare at the clear tubes, the wires and electrode pads, all feeding into the mechanical heart of it. The display screen is black now, waiting to come alive, waiting for someone to feed it their illness. I can see how people would be frightened of it.

They had good cause, once. Many lives were lost trying to replicate that first, accidental Transfer, back in the Victorian Era, when people experimented with blood, electricity, and live volunteers. But these days you only have reason to be afraid if you are on the receiving end.

It started as a purely experimental process, but when a diphtheria epidemic began claiming the children of Edwardian Parliamentarians, the Transfer was a way both to save the children and provide an alternative to the gallows for criminals. So the National Transfer Service was founded.

Tubes and wires lead into the wall behind me, to the other side of St. Barts. The other side of the law. The other side of right and wrong.

After the initial success of the person-to-person Transfer, scientists spent untold fortunes trying to find a way to transfer a disease to animals, to cell cultures, to corpses. But the Transfer can't make a virus jump to other DNA unless it's human, and alive.

I check my phone again. Nine-thirty-four. The Transfer takes about twenty minutes to pump most of my blood through the machine. My body's defences can remove the rest.

I'm relieved when the nurse comes back in. She doesn't look up from her notes.

"You have the start of a rhinovirus. The common cold. You're lucky. There are always people ready who have been sentenced to colds. They've matched you with one."

She turns on the machine and it whirrs into flashing, spinning life. She hooks me up, sticking the cold pads on my skin, pushing a needle roughly into the back of my hand. I don't flinch.

"It'll take about twenty minutes," she says, clearly starting a familiar spiel. "There is no discomfort on this side of the Transfer, although you may feel some odd sensations during the process."

The clear tube fills with red, and she squints at the display, pressing buttons, adjusting dials. The tingle starts, like a shiver running through my blood.

"I'll be back when it's finished," she says, already heading out the door. And then I'm alone again, in the white room, with nothing but the hum of the machine for company, and that odd tickle under the skin that shows the Transfer is working. I don't understand the science, but my headache is fading already as the electricity and magnetism at the heart of the machine transfers my virus through the membrane that separates my blood from that of a criminal.

I wonder who they are. Perhaps it's a shoplifter. Or someone convicted of trespassing. It's unpleasant, receiving a Transfer. I hope it'll give them a shock, enough to realize they're on the wrong path, make them reconsider. It's nice to think my disease might turn someone's life around.

I check the news on my phone. The polls are worse than last week. Dad is eight points behind Sebastian Conway's party. No wonder the team is so low.

I wish I'd brought a book. I miss my social media accounts. But I had to delete those once Dad became party leader. Every time I logged in I found a load of disgusting threats from the criminals that oppose him. So I play games on my phone instead.

When the Transfer is done, the beeping brings the nurse back in. My head is clear, and my throat is wonderfully normal. The nurse checks me over and asks if she should call security to escort me out. I shake my head. Dad would want me to, but it's nine-fifty-six and I don't have time to wait for the guard. I head back to the lift and press the glowing circle of the ground-floor button.

The lift doors open and I step out into the echoing space of the foyer.

It's too quiet. The click of my low heels is the only sound in the hushed entrance. I take in the still tableau by the coffee shop to my right: people frozen, paper cups halfway to their lips. I follow their gaze.

A man stands inside the main door. A meat cleaver gleams in his hand.

CHAPTER TWO

THERE'S THIS THING CALLED *normalcy bias*. Basically, we're so used to everything being okay that if something awful suddenly happens, it can take about eight seconds to clue in. That's much longer than it sounds. People die in earthquakes when they have plenty of time to get to safety. They stand there as the masonry falls around them, trying to process what's happening.

I learned about normalcy bias the hard way, four years ago.

And now, just like back then, I can't move. All I see is the cleaver, clutched between dark brown fingers. The wide blade reflects the clean marble of the lobby.

Meat cleaver. Hospital. Madman. I try to make sense of it.

The atrium springs back to life around me, sound swelling into the vacuum of silence: chairs scraping, voices shouting, the squeak of shoes on the polished floor. But I'm stuck, staring at the black man as he lurches further into the lobby like Frankenstein's monster.

My heart is jammed in my throat, cutting off my breath. I try to remember my self-defense lessons. How are you meant to defend yourself against a man with a blade the size of your head?

I take a few steps back toward the café, trip over a chair, and stumble against a rickety table. I watch as an abandoned coffee tips and the brown liquid arcs through the air, splashing onto the floor.

The man is between me and the front doors, advancing. People are running past him. Has anyone called the police, or security? Where are they? I thought there was a shoot-to-kill policy at hospitals.

That's when I see her. Rebecca. My dead sister, come to life.

She's standing behind the madman with the cleaver. Where did she come from? I feel as if a part of my brain has disconnected. I try to force the scene to make sense.

Madman. Blade. Rebecca. Is history repeating itself?

No. It was a gun last time.

And my heart clenches. It's not Rebecca. Not at all. She's about the same age, but her eyes are green, her skin darker. How could I have mistaken her?

The girl cries out, and the man stops and turns to face her.

You notice more details at a time like this. The glisten of sweat on the man's skin, his chest heaving. The thin crack that threads across the floor of the foyer, connecting me to the girl.

I can get out now. The man's attention is fixed on the girl. I glance around for her family. Where are they? Everyone is flowing away from the two of them, running out the doors or up the stairs.

The girl is frozen, mouth open, as the man lumbers toward her. She starts waving her arms and I wonder what she's doing. Then I realize. She's calling for help.

From me.

The man is close to her now. She's shouting, but I can't hear what over the rush of blood in my ears.

I can't let this happen again.

It's time to move. He's armed. I need a weapon too. I kick off my heels and stand steadier on the smooth floor. I can save this girl. It can be different this time.

Her mouth distorts as she cries out, her eyes fixed on the brute staggering toward her. Tears gleam on her cheeks. There's no time. He's almost reached her, the cleaver tightly clasped in his right fist.

My gaze falls on the café chairs. I lunge toward one and latch on to the metal bar at the top of the backrest. I swing it off the ground. The chair's heavy, but I have momentum on my side. My muscles stretch but I keep my grip as I careen forward, getting closer to the bulk of the man's back.

The reek of him hits me before I'm even close — an animal stink of sweat, of soiled clothes. The dark brown of his scalp shows through his thinning hair. My target.

With a grunt, I swing the chair around, heaving it up as high as I can toward his skull. I close my eyes and pray it will connect.

It does. Hard. The impact knocks the chair out of my grip and it flies off to the side. I duck as it clatters to the floor. The man falls, legs folding beneath him. His head hits the ground with a dull thump. I'm frozen in a protective half-crouch, hands still trembling from the reverberation of the metal when it hit him.

The man lands face down. A trickle of blood leaks from behind his ear, pooling on the white marble. I stare, the anger evaporating.

Oh God, have I killed him?

But the girl is okay. She looks up at me. There are tears on her cheeks. A long moment passes between us.

Before I can move she turns and runs for the doors. I'm about to follow when the man groans and his arm flails toward the cleaver. He's alive.

I kick the blade away from him as the wail of sirens builds outside.

⚡

The police station is over-air-conditioned. Even if it were warmer, I'd still be shaking. At least I have something to blame it on. The shock has kicked in, and goosebumps run along my skin. I jump at raised voices, at doors slamming, even at people talking to me.

The police brought me here. I gave my name to the first officers on the scene, and they whisked me out of there before the press got wind of it. I couldn't reach Dad. He was probably in the middle of the brunch. I managed to get hold of Piers. I didn't make much sense, but I told him which station they were taking me to.

"Did you find the girl?" I ask the blond officer who has been assigned to me. She's sitting opposite me at a desk, finishing up her notes from my statement.

"Not yet." She gives me a sympathetic smile.

The girl was gone when the police burst in. She wasn't Rebecca, didn't even look like her. It was only the shock that gave that momentary illusion. She had darker skin, and her face was thinner, like a little fox. But for a moment as we stared at each other, that didn't matter. For this girl, I moved fast enough. I wasn't too late.

"Where could she have gone? Where was her family?"

"We're looking into it. We'll let you know as soon as we have some information."

"The streets around St. Barts aren't safe. She was scared, vulnerable." I grab hold of the officer's arm. "What if she's wandered into the criminal slums of the Barbican?"

The officer looks down at where I'm holding onto her. I let go.

"Maybe we should take you to an interview room. It'll be safer. Keep you out of the public eye. This way."

She shows me into a room with a gum-stained floor, and gestures toward a plastic chair. In the quiet, the adrenaline drains from my system, leaving me shaking.

"Would you like a cup of tea?" she asks.

I want to say yes. It's something to do with my trembling hands, at least. But instead I burst into tears. The officer looks frightened.

"Are you okay?"

I can't stop crying. I try to say I'm fine, but it comes out in an inaudible mess of snot and tears. The officer approaches me warily, then puts an arm around me.

"There, there," she says, patting my back. "You're safe now."

I know that. I want to stop, but the blubbering continues, accompanied by back-shaking sobs. She must think I'm so pathetic. Finally I'm able to get myself under control, and stop the tears. We stand awkwardly for a moment, her arm still around me, before I pull away. She looks at my face, and from her expression I can tell it's a mess. I'm not wearing waterproof mascara.

"I'll get you a tissue, and that cup of tea," she says.

"Thank you so much," I manage. After she goes, I try to clean myself up a little with my sleeve, leaving black streaks across it.

A few minutes later the officer comes back in with my cup of tea, a handful of tissues, and my dad.

"Look who I found out in the corridor," she says. She's trying to be lighthearted, but it must be weird dealing with the man who may soon be your boss's boss's boss's boss.

I stand up, and my father hurries over, almost knocking the tea from the policewoman's hand. He throws his arms around me and squeezes so tightly he forces the air out of me.

Over Dad's shoulder I see Alison and Piers enter the room. Dad holds me for a minute, then pulls away, looking at my face.

"Oh, Talia," he says, then hugs me again. "I'm so sorry. I'm so sorry," he says, quietly, into my ear. "I should have been there. Again."

"Are you okay?" Alison asks. I nod and she exhales. "Thank God."

"I'm not hurt." I'm glad Dad didn't see my blubbering. He's worried enough already. Hopefully I cleared most of the wreckage of my makeup off my face.

Piers is leaning on his stick and grinning, at me. I've never seen him doing that before. It's kind of weird. I thought he'd be mad that I pulled them away from the Knightsbridge brunch.

Dad turns back to the officer, already his usual composed self. He's still pale, but it could be the fluorescent light.

"Ah, tea," he said, peering at the mug she's holding. "For my daughter, I presume?" He takes it from her and passes it to me. "Thank you so much."

I clutch it and the warmth seeps through my hands.

"Can I get you anything, sir?" she asks, still clutching the tissues.

"If it isn't too much trouble, I could use a tea myself. Just a drop of milk, no sugar."

Dad never remembers to eat or drink unless something is put in front of him, so I know he's trying to get rid of the policewoman, politely. She practically bows on the way out.

Dad waits until the door has clicked shut, then turns to me. "What were you thinking, Talia? You could have been killed."

"Did they tell you about the girl?"

Piers limps forward. "They couldn't stop talking about it! They said you saved her life. This is going to play so well in the media. I could hug you, seriously."

Dad rounds on him. "This isn't a PR stunt, Piers." He turns back to me. "You should've called security to escort you out. What were you thinking? This is the second time I've almost lost you to criminals." He shakes his head. "It's not safe out there."

"You'll fix it," I say. "Make the whole country safer. As soon as you're prime minister"

"It'll take time, Talia. But you have to look after yourself."

"I couldn't leave the girl. She was waving to me for help. She was the same age as Rebecca."

Dad stiffens. "I see. Is she okay?"

"I don't know. She ran away. We have to find her."

"Calm down. You're getting worked up."

"No, I'm not." But I'm speaking too fast. "She can't have been older than nine or ten, and she was all alone at a hospital. It's not right."

"She's not Rebecca. You can't bring her or your mother back."

I shrug his hand off. "I know that, Dad. I just need to check that she's safe. She looked so frightened, so small." I gesture, forgetting about the tea I'm holding, and a wave of it sloshes over the rim and splashes on the floor.

"Talia," Dad says, in his warning voice. He takes what remains of the tea from me and places it on the table. "I'm sure the police are looking into it. I'll ask them to keep us in the loop."

I want to ask for more, want to demand he find her, now. But a little muscle in his cheek twitches, and I know better than to push him. To my surprise, it's Piers who steps in.

"She's right, Malcolm. We have to find her. We'll hold a press conference, tomorrow, and you can launch an appeal. I'm sure she wants to thank Talia for saving her life, and we could get two days of headlines from this, at least. It could be exactly what this campaign needs."

Piers leans his stick against the wall, limps over, and to my surprise, really does hug me.

≠

Dad and Alison's phones start ringing before we even leave the station. I wonder if it's Piers or the police who leaked it. The story breaks on the lunchtime news, and is the top item by the evening. I'm on the cover of most papers the next morning. The tabloids have a field day with it. One calls me "the hero daughter of our next prime minister," then phones Alison and asks if I'll pose topless when I turn eighteen. Dad looks like he wants to punch something when she tells us.

But by the next evening the polls show Dad's popularity is rising. We're back on track.

I even get an invitation to appear on *Sharpe*, Marcus Sharpe's show. Piers and I convince Dad to accept. I'm nervous, but it'll be a softball interview and it could be a huge boost to Dad's campaign. If it goes well, Dad might take me on the campaign trail once Parliament is dissolved. I'm suddenly an election asset, after all.

But I'm agreeing because of the girl. No one has come forward, not even after Dad's press conference, and now I'm worried. And what better way to find her than an appeal on national television?

CHAPTER THREE

"SHE CAN DO HER makeup herself," Piers says.

The girl stops, brush poised over my face. I watch the two of them reflected in the brightly lit mirror backstage at the Sharpe studio.

"The lights in the studio ...," she starts to say.

"Will wash her out," Piers interrupts. "She knows. She'll apply more than usual. It's not rocket science."

The makeup girl looks like a deer caught in the headlights. The brush is still inches from my cheeks, laden with pink powder.

"Why don't you take a break? I'm sure you've been working hard." Piers puts a hand on her back, and turns her toward the door, the blusher brush still in her hand. He follows, leaning on his walking stick. As soon as she's through the door, he closes it gently.

"What was that about?" I ask

"We need some time to talk," Piers says, limping back over. "And she's used to doing makeup for tarty celebrities. You need a more natural look. You can do that, right?"

With the array of brushes and colors in front of me, that shouldn't be a problem. I pick up the tube of foundation closest to my skin tone and try it on the back of my hand.

"What do you want to talk about?"

"What you're going to say in the interview." Piers leans on the back of the chair. "Normally, I'd have given you some proper media training, but we didn't have time."

The shade is a match. I dab it under my eyes and on my chin and nose, then blend it in with a sponge.

"I know what to say. Dad and I have been playing 'interview' for years. The Government is a bunch of crooks, and Sebastian Conway and the Democratic Justice Party will go easy on criminals and reintroduce vaccines. Who wants them sticking needles in the arms of children and babies?"

Piers pats my shoulder. "Those are all great points. But there's a special message you need to convey to the public. And only you can do it."

That's when the door bursts open. The two of us turn as Alison rushes in, breathless.

Great. Who invited her?

"Sorry I'm late," she puffs.

"Late?" Piers says. "I thought you were in meetings with Malcolm."

"He sent me," she says. "He wanted me to make sure Talia is comfortable with this."

I pick up the powder brush and sweep it across my cheek. "I'm fine."

"Good. Good." Alison says.

Piers turns his back on her to meet my eyes in the mirror again.

"You've seen the CCTV footage?"

I nod. He sent it to me earlier. It's terrible resolution, but I do look good in it. Sadly, the girl isn't much more than a grainy black-and-white figure, her back to the camera.

"Excellent," he says. "I was a little worried that might upset you."

"We don't want anything upsetting you," Alison chips in.

"I'm fine," I say.

"She's not a child," Piers says.

I scan the colors in front of me and select a natural-looking brown for my eyeshadow. I don't want to go too "celebrity" with my colors. Piers bends down, closer to my ear. He speaks in a low voice.

"We need to address the Rebecca issue."

Alison leans in to eavesdrop. "Malcolm wants to avoid that."

I fill in the crease of my eyelid and address Piers. "What Rebecca issue?"

"The public knows you as the survivor of a double murder. They see you, they think of your sister and mother. You saved a girl Rebecca's age. Sharpe will want to talk about that."

That didn't occur to me. "What should I do?"

"Play it up," Piers says. "It generates sympathy. Reminds people that Sebastian Conway wants to go easy on criminals, putting us all in the kind of danger you faced."

"This isn't about manipulating voters," Alison says. "This is real."

I put down the makeup brush. "I said I'm fine like a billion times. Treat me like an adult."

"Alison, just because you and Malcolm ...." Piers stops. Alison's face is red.

My stomach lurches. "What?"

Piers shakes his head. "Just don't think you know him best, Alison, is all I'm saying."

I breathe in deeply through my nose. He can't mean ... Dad isn't like that. And Alison is, like, twenty years younger than him.

But I remember the outfit she was wearing two days in a row at our flat.

"The interview should be a cake-walk," Piers says. "Marcus Sharpe is getting too old for celebrity interviews and wants to move into politics. We've offered him an exclusive with your father the night before the election if your interview goes well. So we're expecting easy questions."

I'm glad of the change of subject. Of course Dad arranged this. He's protecting me. He always does. I swallow, and try to push the thought of Alison out of my head.

"So, what's the special message you need me to deliver? Do you have something for me to memorize?" I've seen them training Dad on talking points. It's pretty straightforward. You practise until it sounds natural.

"Special message?" Alison asks.

Piers sighs. I probably shouldn't have said that in front of Alison.

"I can't write it for you," Piers says as I pick up the blusher brush and select a subtle pink. "But our polling has shown that people see your father as too harsh, unsympathetic to the underprivileged."

Alison jumps in again. "But they think he's trustworthy," she says. "They believe he'll do what he says."

I don't want to hear her talking about my dad right now. I grab a lipstick brush and jab it into a healthy reddish tone.

Piers continues. "They think he's cold and distant. But you're in a unique position to counterbalance that."

I laugh. "Cold and distant? Dad?"

"We need you to talk about your father's support after the attack: his visits in hospital, when you were there for so long. I know it was hard for you."

Piers pauses, and I wonder if he's thinking about his own time in hospital. He was there for three months. That's why he needs a walking stick. He was beaten and left for dead by some thug who wanted his wallet. His attacker was sentenced to tuberculosis, but turned out to have natural immunity and was out of Quarantine in two weeks.

Piers shakes his head, continues. "Personal stories, make him seem warmer, more like the dad you know. Can you do that?"

I pause in outlining my lips, and meet Piers's eyes. This isn't just how I should play the interview. This is how I can make myself indispensable to the campaign, get them to take me on the road after Parliament is dissolved. I'm the only person who can let the voters know what my dad is like. That's a lot of responsibility. But an opportunity too.

"No problem," I say.

Piers squeezes my shoulder encouragingly. "You'll be brilliant, Talia. Now get out there and change the world."

"I'll do my best."

⨎

Alison and Piers offer to wait with me in the wings of the *Sharpe* studio. But I don't want Alison around right now, so I tell them I'll be fine.

Standing alone, the weight of the interview settles on my shoulders. This could be key to the campaign, and it's all up to me. I'd be more comfortable with some kind of practised script to rely on. And I can't get Alison out of my head. Gross thoughts seep in as I try to focus on the show.

I'm the last guest and Marcus has been building up to my interview for half an hour, teasing the viewers with hints about the exclusive CCTV footage.

Finally, the floor manager leads me to the edge of the set, and I have a moment to take in the scene. The audience is barely visible behind the blinding lights, but I can make out several rows of filled seats rising in a semicircle around the stage, like an amphitheater.

Marcus is standing in the middle of the studio floor. I can't make out what he's saying, until his voice goes up triumphantly at the end.

"Ladies and gentlemen, Talia Hale!" He points toward the wings, right at me.

I pause for too long, so the floor manager gives me a little push. A whooping, thumping wall of sound rolls in from the audience. Squinting past the lights I can see they're on their feet. People are whistling and clapping their hands above their heads. I push my shoulders back and suck in my stomach as I walk in, smiling at the cameras.

Marcus strides over to greet me. He takes my hand in both of his and shakes it, then gestures to one of the two gray chairs at the heart of the lights, the cameras, the action. I thank him and lower myself into it, smoothing down my red cashmere dress. I wish I'd worn something lighter. It's hot under these lights.

Marcus tries to speak a couple of times, but has to wait for the audience's cheers to fade before he can make himself heard.

It's a little overwhelming. I guess they read the papers, and it's nice, but I'm not sure what I'm supposed to do while they cheer. My chair is angled slightly toward the cameras and the audience beyond. Time stretches out as I clutch my hands together in my lap.

"They like you," Marcus says, gesturing at the crowd. This gets them going again, and Marcus laughs, showing his famous white teeth. We wait until the applause dies down enough for the interview to begin properly.

"So, Talia, what's it like being the daughter of a potential prime minister?"

"It's … it's nice," I stutter. Oh, great start, Talia.

"Nice? In what way?"

"He's nice. He's a good dad." I can hear the words coming out of my mouth, but for some reason I can't stop them, or change them to something less moronic. I try to focus on what Piers told me to say. What only I can say. I swallow, and try again.

"He's always been there for me. Especially four years ago, after the … the attack. He came to visit me in hospital every day."

Marcus is silent, so I continue. My voice grows stronger.

"He's got a great sense of humor."

Marcus's eyebrows rise. I turn to the cameras, speak straight to them.

"You wouldn't know it to see him on TV, but he does. I could barely move, after the attack. But he'd squish up next to me on the hospital bed, his arms warm around me, his beard tickling the top of my head, and watch DVDs."

I swallow. It's still painful to remember those days. "He'd watch my favorites ten times over and never complain. Sometimes, afterwards, he'd stick his socks on his hands like this …," I demonstrate, pinching my fingers against my thumb, making a mouth, "… and re-enact the best parts in funny voices with his sock puppets."

Laughter flows in from the audience. I bet they never imagined him doing that. This is what Piers wanted: a new, friendly view of my father, even if it makes me seem a bit childish.

"He'd spend every moment he wasn't in the Commons with me. He was so tired all the time because of it." I swallow. My mouth is dry, but Marcus smiles, encouragingly.

"One day he dozed off in a committee meeting. The Home Secretary woke him by poking him in the arm with her pen. She broke the skin. Dad has a permanent blue spot on his arm now, a tattoo. You should ask to see it."

A wave of laughter rolls in from the audience, matched by Marcus's loud guffaw. It's a bit too loud, to be honest. He must be desperate for that pre-election interview with Dad.

"And it's good to see that you are just as committed to your father's 'tough on crime' agenda, Talia," Marcus says. "In a more practical way." He turns to the audience. "Shall I show you our exclusive CCTV footage?"

The cheers are so loud Marcus pretends they've pushed him backwards. He holds his hands up, a fake shield. "Okay, okay! Roll the video!"

The lights in the studio dim, the back wall lights up as they run the footage. It's only slightly better than it was on my computer. You still can't tell what the girl looks like, but I hardly hesitate before I rush in to save her.

The lights go up, and I'm still blinking when the cheering starts.

They've put up a freeze-frame of me with the chair, about to hit the man as he advances on the girl, cleaver clutched in his hand. Only the side of my face is visible, but I look way calmer than I felt at the time. I look determined, and strong.

"That, to me, is what true bravery looks like. What were you thinking?"

Wow, he's sucking up a bit too much now. But this is my chance to use Piers's advice.

"She was about Rebecca's age. I wasn't going to let criminals destroy her family the way they destroyed mine."

"And he was quite the criminal too," Marcus says. "He must have been twice your size. He had a long rap sheet. The police have been looking for him for ages."

This is news to me.

"The prosecution is seeking a sentence of bacterial meningitis, as well as a Level 4 Recall. What do you think of that?"

The question blindsides me, even though I know what it means. Almost certain death, and if he survives and there is a pandemic of a serious disease within a year, he'll be recalled to the hospital for a second Transfer. I pause, and try to get my thoughts in order. I don't want to get this one wrong.

"I am sorry for him," I say. "I wish he had made better choices in life. But there was a boy at my school who had meningitis, and might have died if it weren't for the Transfer. In the end, that man," I point at the screen, "may save someone's life. It's a chance to redeem himself. He could have killed the girl."

"It looks like he would have, if you hadn't intervened. She's safe because of you."

"She's not," I say. "She's still missing."

There's a collective "oh" from the audience.

"Missing?" Marcus says.

"I've been trying to find her. It's a dangerous area. She was scared and ran away. But no one's seen her."

"I'm sure someone has seen her. Perhaps she doesn't know people are looking for her. Steve," he says. I squint to try to see who he's talking to, but the lights are too bright. "Do we still have the other footage?"

Marcus presses a finger to the mic in his ear and listens. After a pause, he speaks again. "Great." He puts a hand on my knee. "We have another angle of the attack. You're not in it, but it's a good view of the girl. With your permission, we could screen it now."

What can I say? He should have run this past our people, but he means well, and if I refuse, it'll disappoint the viewers. And how am I going to put out an appeal if the audience don't know what the girl looks like? So I nod, feeling as if my tongue has swollen in my mouth.

A few seconds later, another video flickers up on the screen. The picture is much clearer. It must be the café's footage, as the view is across the foyer. The camera points down slightly, capturing the girl and the crack she stood on, the one that connected her to me. But I'm off-screen, as is the man with the cleaver. It's obvious why they didn't use this footage earlier; none of the action will be on it. But the girl is there, and she's speaking, pleading, waving.

But not to me.

A shiver of sweat tickles its way down my spine. What is going on? Her gaze doesn't follow the line of the crack to where I stood. It falls a little to the right, to where the man was.

Is she waving at him? Why? She freezes, then her hand goes to her mouth. Her eyes are wide now, fearful. She's looking at me for the first time. Then she turns and runs, out of the shot, out of the hospital.

The lights go up in the studio, catching me by surprise. There's more applause and I smile at the audience. The crack wasn't visible in the other, low-quality video. They couldn't have known she wasn't waving to me.

I hope my grin looks genuine. It's about to peel off my face.

"Well, there you go. That's the missing girl."

I nod mechanically. Why was she trying to get the man's attention? Why did she look so frightened after I knocked him out?

"What did you think when you saw her waving at you like that?"

Silence fills the studio as his question hangs in the air. I need to order my thoughts. People in the audience lean forward, the pale ovals of their faces appearing out of the shadows. There are so many of them, waiting for me to speak.

She wasn't waving at me. She was waving at the man.

"I acted on instinct," I manage, but my voice trembles. "She must have been scared."

Could that be it? Perhaps she was focused on him in her panic.

"I'm sure she was terrified," Marcus says. "Who knows what might have happened if you hadn't been there."

I'm losing this. I need to keep it together. The freeze-frame on the screen behind me draws my attention. I sit there, staring at the shock in the girl's face after I knocked out the man.

Marcus comes to my rescue. He addresses the cameras directly. "If you know the girl, please get in touch with us, or the police."

He pats my knee again. "Over four million viewers watch this show. We'll find her." He turns back to the viewers. "Well, sadly that's all we have time for today. But I think you'll agree, whatever party you support, that Talia Hale is an exceptional young woman."

He shakes my hand as the audience rises to a standing ovation. Was that enough? Someone must know her. Someone will find her. And even if they don't, I remember what I saw in her expression, who she was facing.

I know where to start looking for her.

CHAPTER FOUR

The clouds are low over London: gray blobs that look as heavy as the concrete-colored Thames below. From the window of our penthouse, it's as if I could reach up and touch them. I imagine how they would feel: like cold sponges.

Rain will soon fall on the city. Fall on the traffic snarled up on Southwark Bridge, fall on Bankside Pier, fall and disappear into the Thames.

I miss our old home, in Notting Hill, the people I knew there. But we couldn't stay in that house. Couldn't sleep in a space haunted by such violence, such regret. I'd find myself back in Mum and Dad's bathroom, wishing I'd moved faster. Remembering how I'd let my sister die.

On afternoons like this I drift around like a ghost myself. I try to read a book, try to do some online coursework for my A-levels, but can't concentrate. The floor-to-ceiling windows mean our home reflects the weather, capturing and amplifying its mood. The cream furniture is cast in gray, the white walls darkened.

The buzz of the lock signals my father's return home. I head for the door as a voice erupts into the flat. Piers's. I can tell by the outrage in his tone, and the clack of his cane.

"Conway has been bandying about that old crap about harsh sentencing and unnecessary Recalls to cut waiting lists. But some criminals are immune to virtually everything, so we need to provide more of a deterrent ..."

And behind Piers is ...

"Dad!" I say as he enters.

"Darling." Dad drops his briefcase and runs to hug me.

Alison enters behind him and I stiffen. She gives me a patronizing grin as she picks up his stuff. I turn away from her and bury my head in my father's shoulder.

"I missed you," I say, quietly, so the others won't hear.

Dad squeezes me and whispers in my ear, "Missed you too." Then he pulls away, unbuttons his long black coat, and hangs it up.

"Are you hungry?" he asks. "We should order sushi. It's still your favorite, right? We're celebrating."

Excitement jolts through me. "You found her?"

Dad tilts his head. "Who? Oh, the girl." He walks to his office; an alcove separated from the main room by a large bookcase. "No, sorry." Alison catches my eye, but I look away, quickly. She follows Dad in like a puppy, thumps his briefcase down on the desk, clicks it open and pulls out some papers with colored bar graphs on them.

"Look, Talia. These are the latest poll numbers." She spreads the papers on his desk. Dad walks around them, straightening the sheets. That's his version of uncontrollable excitement.

I glance down. All the big names are there. Ipsos MORI, Angus Reid, YouGov. And they're all saying the same thing. I look up, and into my father's beaming face.

"We're neck-and-neck with Sebastian Conway," Alison says.

I ignore her and give Dad another hug, squeezing his skinny frame. This is what he wants more than anything.

"You're finally getting through to people!"

When I release him, he ruffles my hair. "I have you to thank for this. Your heroics have got a lot of attention."

There's a swell in my chest. "We're a team," I say.

Piers starts tidying the papers. "It's only neck and neck. There are margins for error. And we shouldn't be jinxing it by celebrating."

"Oh, take the stick out of your arse, Piers," Alison says. "Let us have this one."

I trail a finger along the edge of the desk. I need to talk to Dad alone, but these days I never get the chance.

He catches my expression. "And what do you want?"

"You said you'd help me find the girl."

"Talia, I've tried. And you've tried. On national TV, no less."

"But we haven't found her."

"That means she probably doesn't want to be found."

"Remember on the news when that child was kidnapped right outside the Barbican by that pedophile ring? What if she's in danger?"

Piers sniffs. "I don't get why this is so important to you. She's probably a criminal."

"She's a child! She can't be more than ten!"

"Talia." Dad sinks into his seat, and I notice the dark circles under his eyes.

Piers keeps talking. "She was there alone. We'd have found her by now if she was there innocently. She was probably picking pockets. She may be under a Recall, and trying to go off grid in case of a pandemic. When your father and I were lawyers, we saw a lot of children her age come through the courts."

"Then she needs to be taken into care. She should be raised by people who'll look after her properly. If she's picking pockets now, what will she be doing when she's older?"

Dad shakes his head. "When they're raised to crime, there's not much we can do. But once we have the right policies in place, this country will be safer. We'll help more than one child that way."

I bite my lip. This is going to be a hard sell. "There's someone else we can ask. About where she is, I mean."

His brow furrows. "Who?"

"The man with the cleaver. When I saw the CCTV, it looked like she was waving to him. He might know where to find her. I want to speak to him."

"Talia!" Dad stands and walks into the sitting room, forcing me to follow him. "That's out of the question."

"But we have to find her."

He turns around, and clutches my arms, making me look into his eyes. "I've almost lost you to criminals twice, Talia. I cannot risk losing you. You're everything to me."

"Quarantine is safe. There's tons of guards and security."

Pier's voice chimes in from behind me. "It would look bad. Consorting with sick people, I mean. Especially ones in Quarantine."

I keep facing Dad. "It would only take a letter from you. Permission from the inmate or an MP, right?"

"I would never send you into that kind of place. End of conversation."

I slump down onto the couch.

Dad sighs. "Can't we have a relaxing night?"

How can we have a relaxing night with his staff here?

"I have to do something this time."

Dad joins me on the couch, putting his arm around me. "You did do something. You saved her. And you can't keep blaming yourself for what happened four years ago. Thomas Bryce was insane. A criminal. You were only twelve, and if you'd done any more I might have lost you, too."

His eyes go to where my scar lies, hidden by my hair, and he swallows.

I shake my head. "This isn't about that. I should have followed that girl out of the hospital. Should have checked she was okay."

Alison wanders into the room, and sits down on the couch next to me. She places a cold hand on my arm. "You stayed and waited for the police. It was the right thing."

I shift so she's no longer touching me.

"I saw the footage, Talia," Dad says. "I know how this must have affected you. When I saw that girl, I felt ... I thought ..."

My father is rarely lost for words, so I turn to him. His eyes glisten. I don't want him to say any more, so I lean over and hug him. He squeezes me tightly to him.

"If there were anything I could to do to bring her back. To bring both of them back." He speaks in a whisper. After a long moment of silence, he straightens up, releases me.

"But we'll save other families, once we're in power. And this girl is not Rebecca." He smoothes his beard. "Why don't you come into Parliament tomorrow? It's the last day before it'll be adjourned for the election. You can do your coursework while we're in the Commons, and I'll get to see more of you that way."

"Malcolm," Piers interjects again. "It's going to be a busy day ..."

"I'll come. I'll stay out of the way when you need me to." It would be nice to spend a bit of time with Dad, even if I'd be alone in his office for most of the day.

His office. Alone.

An idea forms in my mind. I'd have access to his letterhead, his printer. Dad might not want me to go to Quarantine, but that's because he's overprotective. He'd be happy to know the girl was okay too. I saw his face when he talked about her. Saw he was as moved as I was.

It would be so easy.

CHAPTER FIVE

PARLIAMENT IS BEING ADJOURNED today, ahead of the election. It's the end of the current government's term, so this is just a formality, and we're really only here for the interviews on College Green afterwards. But in the meantime, Dad's in meetings, strategizing with his cabinet, popping back to his office when he can, bringing hot chocolate or biscuits for me. But mostly I'm left to myself.

I've got loads of coursework to do. I'm normally more on top of it. Ever since Mum and Rebecca were murdered, I've been home-schooled. Dad used to teach me himself, too paranoid to send me to school. We worked well together. But as he rose through the ranks of the National Law Party he got busier and busier. These days I take care of my own education. There are loads of online programs. It's no problem.

But today my attention slides from the history essay on my laptop to the portraits on the wall, to the dust motes dancing in the late afternoon light from the window. There's more history in this building than I could ever fit in my essay. I'm probably breathing in Winston Churchill's skin cells right now. I should get marks for that.

My gaze falls on my father's stationery, already loaded in his printer. That's all I need, a letter. Relatives can visit, and people who've been invited by the prisoners, but I'd need special permission. A letter from my MP would be enough.

I'm waiting for the right time. I'd be in so much trouble if he caught me, but it'll be safe once he's in the Commons.

I don't want to see the man with the cleaver. He'll probably scream at me, threaten me. I doubt he'll help. But how else am I going to find the girl?

There's a photo sitting on Dad's desk. The four of us on holiday in Venice, five years ago. We're in St. Mark's Square, early in the morning when it was almost deserted, beaming for the camera. Me, Dad, Mum, and Rebecca. I can't take my eyes from my sister. She was eight then, with only a year left to live.

I jump as the door opens. Dad pops his head in. "Everything okay?"

Piers's voice comes from behind him, arguing with someone, as usual.

"Fine, Dad." I hope my thoughts don't show on my face.

"We're heading into the chamber now. Is there anything you need? Snacks? Help with your work?"

I press my lips together and shake my head. "No, thanks."

I catch a glimpse of Piers in the hallway, wagging his finger at an unseen victim.

Dad continues. "How about afternoon tea? After the interviews?"

Hope surges through me. There's a gap in his calendar. I saw it. But gaps have a way of closing.

"Will Piers let you?"

Dad glances over his shoulder. "I'll convince him."

"I'll believe it when I see it."

"Malcolm!" Piers's voice. "It's time."

"I'll see you later." Dad ducks out and shuts the door.

The footsteps outside build to a hurrying crescendo, then slowly peter out. I guess they're all in the Commons now. Silence descends over the sunlit room.

Now is the time.

I open a new document, and start typing as fast as I can. "I, Malcolm Hale, Leader of Her Majesty's Opposition, give permission for my daughter and constituent, Talia Hale, to visit …"

I stop. I forget his name. I must have seen it, in the news. But I've been so focused on the girl it hasn't stuck in my mind.

I open my browser and search. The first result is an article in the *Guardian*.

"Jack Benson (40), a resident of the Barbican with a long criminal record, known by the street name 'Hippo' …"

That's an odd alias. I guess it's because he's so big. But the Barbican makes sense. It's filled with criminals. Even the police fear to tread in that architectural monstrosity they dropped in the middle of the city. It's where Mum and Rebecca's killer lived.

My fingers find their places on the keyboard again.

"… to visit Jack Benson, in Quarantine. Yours sincerely," I hit enter a few times to leave space for the signature, "Malcolm Hale, MP."

The door swings open. I slam my computer shut.

It's Alison. She peers around the door. "Hi, I'm looking for Malcolm. Have they gone to the Commons already?"

I nod.

"Thanks!" She closes the door behind her. I reopen and restart my laptop, cursing Alison under my breath. Thank goodness for autosave. The letter reappears on the screen.

I glance at the picture of my family, of Mum and Rebecca. A familiar hollowness radiates through me. The sense of something missing, every day, for four years. The sense of a life that broke in two, and healed back badly.

Maybe I can fix someone else's family, at least.

I take a deep breath and click on "Print."

I jump as the printer quietly whirrs into action. I stand up, creep to the door and check the corridor. The carpet runs down the long hallway, between the portraits, the wood paneling. It's empty. I duck back into my father's office and close the door.

I pick up the letter from the printer. Perfect. The official feel of the thick paper stock, the green portcullis letterhead with the crown on top. I need his signature, but I've seen that enough times to be able to fake it.

Footsteps outside, the murmur of voices. I fold the letter in half and slide it under my computer.

The door opens.

Dad's frowning. "Talia," he says, striding over. How does he know?

I notice, almost too late, that I still have the letter open on my screen. I lunge for the computer and click on the "x" in the corner and my heart stops when a window springs open.

Do you want to save your changes?

I jab at the mouse pad, selecting "No." The window closes as Dad reaches my side.

"Computer trouble?" he says.

"Nope. Just saving my essay." I'm surprised my voice sounds so calm. "You can't be done already."

"No, sweetpea. I wanted to let you know I spoke —"

Piers's voice from outside. "Come on, Malcolm."

I look up into Dad's face, but he avoids my eyes. My shoulders slump.

"Piers said no to afternoon tea."

Dad inhales through his teeth. "I'm so sorry. Can we go out this evening instead? Piers is right, unfortunately. I have to be there to rally the backbenchers before they go back to their constituencies."

"You have a fundraiser tonight, Malcolm," Piers says, peering through the door.

I let my gaze fall to my computer. The corner of the letter is sticking out. I want to nudge it back in, but that might draw attention to it.

"Sorry, darling. I'll make it up to you. It'll be calmer after the election."

I see my opportunity. "Fine. I'll go out and get some food now."

"You can get tea in one of the cafes. The Terrace, or the Jubilee. Or I'll get someone to bring you anything you like." He's almost pleading.

"I'd like to go for a walk along the Thames. Go somewhere on the South Bank. It's a beautiful day."

Dad tenses. "I'd rather you stayed in the Palace of Westminster. After everything —"

"And I'd rather we got afternoon tea together." I'm being mean, but I need to get out. I'm sick of sitting in this room, sick of wandering the antique hallways under the judgmental glare of the statues and portraits. Quarantine would feel healthier than this.

"I'll get Mike to drive you," he says.

"Don't be paranoid, Dad. I want to walk."

"She'll be fine, Malcolm. But we have to go," Piers says.

Dad rummages in his pocket and pulls out his wallet. He produces a £50 note. "Stay close by. And wear your hat and sunglasses."

"Yes, Dad." I take the money. "Full disguise. I get it."

Dad doesn't move.

"Come on, Malcolm!" Piers says.

Dad moves toward me, reaches his arms out to hug me, but I turn to the side, so he ends up patting me on the shoulder, awkwardly. "I love you Talia."

"I know."

"Now, Malcolm." Piers waves toward the door. And with that, they're gone. Leaving me alone, staring at the white paper peeking out from under my computer.

When I'm sure the coast is clear, I pull it out, and choose a pen from the organizer on Dad's desk. I take a deep breath, then loop my way through the familiar consonants and vowels of Dad's name. I hold it up to the afternoon sunlight and admire my forgery.

It's perfect.

CHAPTER SIX

BRIDGE STREET,
LONDON
NINETEEN DAYS LEFT

IT'S ANOTHER BLUSTERY DAY. Leaves blow against me, sticking to my coat as I try to flag down a black cab. At least it's bright out. I feel stupid with sunglasses on when it's cloudy. But I've learned to wear them anyway, viewing London in a murky gray, as if still smothered by Victorian smog. Living in a twilight world is better than getting hassled on the street by fans and foes of my father. I've had people swear in my face.

A cab finally pulls up and I settle into the rounded interior.

"Where to, love?"

"Holloway Quarantine."

The cabbie's eyebrows rise in the rearview mirror, but he puts the car in gear, and pulls away from the curb. I settle back in my seat and watch the city pass me by.

Doubt creeps in as we crawl through the traffic and head north, leaving behind the London that tourists see. But I'm not afraid of Jack Benson. He can't hurt me now. I'm more worried that he'll refuse to help, refuse to tell me what he knows.

It's a long drive, but eventually I see Quarantine appear ahead of us. I watch the fortress grow through the front window of the cab until I can pick out the different gray and white bricks decorating the turrets.

"Here we are then," the cabbie says.

I pay the fare, tip well, and shuffle out of the car. The cabbie has dropped me by the visitors' entrance. A woman is at the gate ahead of me, stooped as she speaks to a guard in his booth. She's wearing a short skirt with heels and a puffer jacket. Her legs must be cold.

The woman enters, and the guard calls, "Next!"

His gaze is on me. I don't move.

"Come on, then."

I feel as if I'm on rails, pulled toward the gate.

"ID," he says. He's young, not more than twenty. "I haven't got all day."

I take off my sunglasses, pull out the letter and hold it toward him. He takes it and his lips move a little as he reads it. Then his eyes widen. He jams his finger down on a button. There's a buzz and a click at the gate.

"Sorry, miss; should have recognized you," he says, standing poker-straight. For a horrible moment I think he's going to salute.

"Thank you."

As I pass the booth the guard picks up a phone. A jolt passes through me. Who is he ringing? Is he checking the letter is genuine? Maybe it's not too late to walk away from all this. But the gate slams shut behind me. I'm locked into a short corridor, bordered on both sides by high chain-link fences topped with razor wire. About ten paces toward the prison is another gate.

I straighten my spine and push my shoulders back. My heels clack on the paving stones until I reach the second gate. It's a long time before there's another buzz and click and it opens in front of me.

The guard on this side has already stepped out of his booth. "Miss Hale," he says. "Welcome to Holloway Quarantine."

"Thank you."

"My colleague," he waves toward the young guard at the first gate, "has requested an escort for you."

The tension in my shoulders unknots a little. Of course I need an escort. They can hardly stick the next prime minister's daughter in the regular visiting rooms. But I'm drawing more attention to myself than I'd planned.

A guard comes out from the main gate. His uniform is smarter, and he's probably in his fifties. His mustache reminds me of a World War I flying ace. He holds out a hand: bright pink, like his face.

"Principal Quarantine Officer Watson," he says. "But you can call me Frank, Miss Hale."

"Nice to meet you, Frank," I say, wincing while his sausage-like fingers crush my hand. "Please, call me Talia."

He turns toward the building. "This way." As we head toward it, he sweeps a hand in front of him, indicating the whole prison.

"I don't know if you know much about Holloway," he says, "but it used to be a women's prison. They were even executed here."

I nod, trying not to shiver. It's hard to imagine that Londoners were ever so barbaric that we thought justice meant killing one person without saving another.

He continues with his guided tour, chest puffed out.

"Once the Transfer became widespread after World War II, long sentences became a thing of the past. So the other prisons closed, one by one. Holloway was converted to London's Quarantine, to keep those awaiting trial and those sentenced to more serious illnesses away from the public and each other while they endure their punishment."

I know all this. But it seems rude to say so. "I see."

"It's also where we keep the offenders who are under Level 4 Recalls. They have a tendency to run instead of reporting to hospitals if a Level 4 Pandemic is declared."

I can see why they would. A Level 4 Pandemic is rare, but it means an outbreak of a deadly illness, like meningitis, TB, or hantavirus pulmonary syndrome.

He approaches yet another gate, nods at a security camera, and brandishes a pass at a black sensor. The gate swings open, and he waves me through, into a white room with a desk along one side and an officer sitting behind it.

"Stand here." He indicates two footprint stencils on the floor and I do as I'm told. He points to a camera mounted on the desk in front of me. "Look in here, please."

There's a click before I can react. Great. There goes any chance I have of denying this if Dad finds out.

"And if you could sign here, miss."

My hand is shaking when I scrawl my name.

"Don't worry," he says, misinterpreting my nervousness. "There's no disease in this wing of Quarantine. We keep the prisoners awaiting trial in isolation and well away from those who are serving their sentences. Can't have them getting sick before they've been found guilty!"

He gives a braying laugh.

In the next room, he takes my jacket and bag, and gives me blue plastic overalls to put over my clothes, like the ones forensic teams wear. They catch on my heels as I pull them on. I'm fitted with a white face mask he calls a respirator. He tightens the elastic straps on my chin and face, then pulls one over his mouth.

"Just a general precaution," he says, voice slightly muffled. "Jack Benson hasn't been sentenced, and there will be glass between you and him."

The suit and mask are oddly reassuring. I feel anonymous as he leads me through more gates, more doors, more checkpoints, all stinking of industrial disinfectant. Finally, we reach a room at the end of a long corridor and he ushers me in. There's a plastic orange chair facing a thick panel of glass. A phone receiver hangs next to it. On the other side I see an empty room, with a matching phone and chair. There's no way Jack Benson will be able to reach me.

Still, I brace myself. Will he recognize me?

The door opens and my whole body tenses.

But the man who slumps in, led by a warden in an orange protective suit, is nothing like the monster with the cleaver. His shoulders are rounded, his head hangs forward, a bald patch at the top.

The warden leads him to the chair and he collapses into it. He looks up at me from under his brow, like a child caught lying. The warden puts the phone receiver in his hand, and I pick up the one on my side.

The man studies my face for a moment. His eyes are clouded with confusion, not the rage I expected, the hate I saw in the eyes of Mum and Rebecca's killer.

Jack Benson sits up straight. "Tig…. Tig, is that you?" He shakes his head, as if to clear it. "No." There's a pleading in his expression. "Is she coming? My daughter? Or Kieron?"

"You have children?" This wasn't what I was expecting. He's well spoken. And I certainly didn't imagine him as a father.

A quizzical expression spreads across his face. "I saw her … Tig, I mean. At the place …." He trails off. His brow knots. "The place!" He's agitated now. "With the … the tables, the marble …."

Cold creeps through my veins. He shakes his head and rests his head in his hands, pushing at the skin with his fingertips.

"I don't remember."

It feels like something is stuck in my throat. I swallow. No, it couldn't be. He's black. The girl at the hospital wasn't, was she? She did have dark skin, but not as dark as his. But if her mother were white …. My insides twist.

"At the hospital," I say. I have to pause, take a deep breath. It's hard to suck air in, through this mask. "At the place …. The girl was your daughter?"

He nods. "Little Tig. I think she was looking for me."

I stare at him for a moment as I remember how the girl seemed to be pleading with him and the horror in her eyes when I hit him with the chair.

"She was your daughter? You weren't going to hurt her?"

"Hurt her? No! I …." His eyes lose focus. "I got lost, I think." He rubs a hand over his big forehead. "I wasn't meant to be out."

The mask is suffocating me. There's something not right about Jack Benson. The way he phrases things. He talks too slowly. I turn to Frank.

"Is he drugged?"

Frank shakes his head. "Was like this when he got here."

I remember the impact of the chair, reverberating through my hands. The blood leaking from his head as he lay on the floor. Did I do this? Did I give him brain damage?

I swallow the bile that rises to my mouth.

"This is Quarantine, isn't it?" Jack Benson says, drawing my attention back to him. He stares at the wall, the ceiling, at the phone in his hand. "No, I can't be here." He starts rocking in the chair, a violent motion.

"Tig," he says. "Take care of Tig. She has no mother."

My mouth opens and closes. She also has no father now, or as good as. Thanks to me.

"Where is she? Tig, I mean?"

"At home. Isn't she?" He's rocking faster. His eyes are wide now.

"I think that's enough," the warden says, behind him.

"Where's home?"

Jack looks around, panicked, then turns back to me. "Shakespeare."

"Miss Hale, he's getting worked up."

"One minute, please." I lean forward. "Shakespeare? What do you mean?"

"Promise." Jack Benson slaps the glass. "Promise to take care of Tig!"

"Of course," I say, quietly. It's the least I can do. Although I have no idea how to keep my promise.

"Come away from there, miss." Frank is standing right behind me, but I can't move.

Jack didn't hear me. "Promise," Jack stands up, drops the phone. But he's shouting, and it still picks up his voice. "Promise you'll look after Tig!"

He punches the glass, and I push backwards, knocking over my chair and virtually falling into Frank's arms. The warden in the other room hits a button on the wall, and the screech of an alarm fills my ears.

"No, wait!" I say.

Jack's still shouting, his mouth moving, forming her name, but I can't hear over the noise. Uniformed men rush in, in full hazmat suits. One shoots a Taser, and the big man collapses to the floor, body jerking.

I stand by my fallen chair, the alarm screaming around me, and I want to shout too. Frank has my arm, he's trying to pull me toward the door, but I slip from his grasp, move back to the window, press my hands against it, shake my head. But no one on that side is paying attention to me. Their focus is on the man on the ground.

A hand on my shoulder makes me jump. I spin around to see Frank, eyes wide with concern above his mask.

"I'm sorry you had to see that, miss."

"His daughter," I say. "The girl was his daughter!" I point at the men surrounding him. "Make them stop! Make them let him go!"

He shakes his head, sadly. I'm being stupid. They aren't going to release him on my say-so. I pull off the mask. I'm too dizzy with it on. I lean my forehead against the wall and try to breathe. There's been a mistake. A big one.

"I don't think he wanted to hurt her. Can we get the charges dropped?"

Frank puts a hand on my back, steers me toward the door. "He's not just up for the hospital incident. He's got a rap sheet as long as my arm, going way back. Drug dealing, mostly. And he assaulted a police officer on the way to Quarantine."

I force a breath in. In the other room, one of the wardens wheels in a gurney, and three of them struggle to lift him onto it.

Frank keeps talking. "You caught a wanted man. You saw how violent he got."

He had a cleaver at the hospital. That's true. Who knows what he was like before I hit him? His daughter might not have been safe around him.

They flop him, face up, onto the bed, and busy themselves with straps and restraints. I turn away, and walk through the door Frank is holding open for me.

"Are you okay, miss? I'm sorry about what happened. Please tell your father it isn't usually like this."

My breath stops in my throat. Dad cannot find out I was here.

"It's ... it's fine. These things happen with criminals. I won't worry my father over this. He's very busy. And you don't need to explain about my visit. To anyone."

Frank's eyes crinkle with a relieved smile. "Thank you, miss."

♯

I feel sick on the drive back through the bustle of London. Worried about Jack Benson. Worried about Tig, and worried about Dad finding out about my trip. At least Frank wanted to keep it under wraps. But I got him to promise to tell Jack Benson's lawyer that Tig is his daughter, and to get a doctor or a psychologist to examine him. Hopefully he'll get a lighter sentence. Get medical treatment.

I stare blankly at the crowds, the shops, the restaurants that flash past the window. Tig has no mother. Not much of a father either, now. And that's my fault.

I've put my sunglasses back on, even though I feel stupid wearing them in the car. They help to hide my red eyes, the tears that keep coming.

The cab pulls up outside Parliament. I pay the driver, and head through the crowds of milling tourists, trying not to walk into them as they weave across the pavement, taking photographs. I have to keep my promise to Jack Benson. Have to find his daughter, get her taken into care, adopted by a good family. I owe him that much, after what I did to him. I'll have to find his address and start searching for her.

I stop. I already know where he lived. A man walks into me and I mutter an apology as I remember the article in the *Guardian*. Jack Benson lived in the Barbican.

That's where I have to go; that's where I have to look for Tig: the slums of the Barbican Estate, where the police fear to tread.

Where Mum and Rebecca's killer lived.

CHAPTER SEVEN

GETTING AWAY FROM DAD and his staff is the easy part. I tell them I'll study at home. Dad agrees, promises afternoon tea another day. Tells me how much he misses me and to call him or his staff if I need anything.

But I can't wander into the Barbican dressed in a Burberry coat and tweed skirt. It would stand out like a bikini in winter. So I head for Oxford Street and get buffeted by the crowds as I work my way to the cheapest of the chain stores. I grab an ensemble modeled on the woman I saw ahead of me at Holloway: pink jacket, short denim skirt, tight T-shirt and cheap trainers. I add a leopard-print Stetson and a scarf I can pull over my face to act as a makeshift mask. I decide to wear my Dior sunglasses. People will assume they're knockoffs, and I need one thing that's still me.

I get changed at home and adjust my makeup, layering on too much eyeliner and drawing wider lips over my own in bright red. I reshape my cheeks with bronzer, curl and back-comb my hair, then shove the hat on top.

I'm a total mess, but I don't even recognize myself. For a second, I feel weightless. I could be anyone: someone normal, someone who doesn't have to behave, who doesn't have to talk politics to everyone she meets. I twirl and laugh.

Unfortunately, I didn't count on the rain. It begins halfway across Southwark Bridge, a stubborn drizzle that fogs up the view and saturates clothing. By the time I reach London Wall my bare legs are freezing, the water running down them and into my trainers, which squeak with each step.

The nearest entrance to the Barbican is a passageway between two buildings, half in shadow below a concrete walkway. Cardboard boxes huddle under the walkway, but the wind blows the rain sideways, and they're as wet as I am.

I take a deep breath, and remind myself I'm doing this for Tig. What if she's living rough in the Barbican? I peer into the boxes as I pass, but she's not there. Just adult-sized lumps under thin blankets.

I head under the walkway, trying to look like I know where I'm going. How do criminals walk? I add a swagger to my step, but I splash in the puddles and it feels wrong.

To my left is some of the original Roman London Wall. It's crumbling now, camouflaged with graffiti: bright orange obscenities sprayed on our ancient history. Disgusting.

It's surrounded by a mess of old tents and lean-tos made of cardboard and plastic, tarpaulins flapping in the wind. My trainers slip in the wet mud, and cupped hands reach out as I pass, mumbled requests for money, for a smoke, for alcohol. I'm still too well dressed for this place. My clothes are new and clean, unlike the filthy shirts that hang off the men clustered around here. Everyone is coughing or sneezing. The smell, the squalor, the clamor for money threatens to overwhelm me.

But I keep my head down through the park, heading for the Barbican itself.

It was meant to be beautiful when it was first planned. But as St. Barts expanded in the sixties, everyone respectable moved away from the beggars, drug dealers, and alcoholics who crowded around the hospital, waiting for their fellow gang members or addict customers to be let back out with diseases too minor to warrant a stay in Quarantine.

So the Barbican became where no-hopers ended up. A place people could hide. Walls were erected around much of the estate, the entrances narrowed and the flats divided in two.

I have to hide my surprise as I step out from the park.

It's a city. A whole city, within the city. Buildings rise up on all sides. Concrete grids of identical windows, tiny gray balconies, rain running down from them. Pollution-stained high-rises, supported on columns, dank paths like tunnels underneath. A dirty labyrinth of walkways, columns, ledges, balconies and flats, intersecting with each other and looming over me.

I'm staring up so much I almost trip walk into a stinking concrete trough. There are dozens, lining the walkway. I guess they were meant to be planters when this place was designed, but it's obvious from the stench they're used as open-air latrines.

The path takes me between two buildings. I step out into a grubby courtyard, surrounded on all sides by the brutal high-rises.

There's an empty fountain in the center, in use as a tatty market, filled with people. I can blend in better there. A crate has been placed at the edge to act as a step down. I tread on it gingerly and climb into the market. Threadbare clothes, filthy tomatoes, dog-eared and soaking paperbacks are laid out on scraps of plastic, someone sitting behind each heap, as people mill around the rudimentary stalls. One woman has four plucked pigeons presented in front of her, and appears to be haggling with a man offering her an old pair of shoes. Her face is covered in a bright red rash.

Men and women are coughing, and noses are being wiped with dirty scraps of cloth. I tighten my scarf around my face and jump as someone sneezes right behind me. These people don't need to be sentenced to diseases; they must pass them around like sweets. No wonder so many of them are immune to what they're sentenced to. It makes a mockery of the whole justice system.

It was dumb to come here. I thought I could walk around for a while and keep an eye out for Tig. I thought I could ask people where Jack used to live, pretend I was a friend. But I stand out too much. And I'm going to catch something here.

Men whistle at me as I go by.

"Oooh," one coos, "fancy lady." There's a hand on my bottom. I spin around, but there are too many people behind me. It could be any one of them.

There must be another way to find the girl, a safer way. There's another crate here, a step out of this nightmarish market. I slip in my haste to get out. Where's the exit? I've been spun around, I don't know which way is south. I'm hemmed in on all sides by the graffiti-strewn walls of the estate, by the foggy rain, by the people and the smell of sweat, the sour scent of alcohol on breath, their broken-teeth leers and dirty hands. The air here is a miasma of germs.

My breath comes hard now. My gaze swings from person to person. They're too close, coughing and sniffing, criminals I'd cross the road to avoid. Killers, like Thomas Bryce. There's a hand in my pocket. I don't react. What if the thief is armed and waiting for an excuse to attack?

Ahead of me, someone walks with purpose, cutting a path through the crowd. His shoulders are back, chin high like he owns the place. His jeans are clean, his jacket new. He's familiar, and I dive through the crowd toward him, as if to a long-lost friend.

He's young, not that much older than me. He says something in acknowledgment to a man he passes, turning around so his face is visible; his brown skin, his green eyes.

I stop.

I've seen him before. It takes a moment for the memory to click into place: the hospital. He looked in my room, asked if I'd seen a big man. I blathered at him, and he moved on.

I put my hand to my mouth. I'd forgotten all about that. But it's obvious now. He was looking for Jack Benson.

His green eyes are as startling as they were then.

Tig has green eyes, too. Could he be the "Kieron" Jack mentioned in Quarantine?

I follow him. It's not like I have any better options. If he's Tig's brother, maybe he's going home. He could lead me right to her. If he isn't, he's still the most normal-looking person in this place, and he clearly knows where he's going.

If he's sensible, it's out of here.

I move into the gap he leaves behind him in the crowd, and match his pace. I keep focused on his feet as they pad along the gum-stained ground. He's wearing high-street trainers, which I guess is expensive for here. How does he make his money? Sensible employers won't touch a resident of the Barbican, for obvious reasons.

Maybe he's a drug dealer, like Jack Benson. I let some distance grow between us. He was sneezing at the hospital. Perhaps he wasn't there to have a Transfer. Perhaps he was receiving one.

He's heading for one of the taller towers. The balconies condense the drizzle into proper rain, and throw it down onto our heads. The boy reaches the door, a spider's web of smashed glass held together by masking tape. He swings it open and disappears into the darkness of the foyer. I grab the stained and loose handle and hesitate.

A man under a drenched blanket nearby is staring at me, his face as filthy as the sheet that covers him. He leers at me, sits up fast, and reaches for my ankle. I yank it away. He breaks into a coughing fit, not even bothering to cover his mouth. I pull the door open hastily and follow the boy inside, out of range of the man's germs.

The glass rattles as the door closes behind me. I pull off my sunglasses but it still takes my eyes a few seconds to adjust. Most of the windows have been replaced by plywood, blocking out the sun. The stench of urine reaches me, and there's liquid on the brown tiled floor. I retch.

A bang to my left draws my attention to a stairwell, the door slamming shut. The boy obviously went that way. I glance over at the lifts, but one set of doors opens into the shaft itself, and the second appears to have been beaten inward. The third set has "out of order" written in spray paint. I should get out of here, get out of the Barbican. But the front door starts to open again, and I'm terrified it's the man with the blanket. I can't let him corner me in here.

I follow the boy.

The stairwell smells worse than the foyer. I avoid a brown lump in the corner. Who uses hallways as loos?

The boy's trainers scuff on the stairs above me. I follow, keeping my eyes on the ground, avoiding the stains and wet patches as much as I can. I'm going to throw my shoes away as soon as I get home, burn them, if I can. My thighs start to ache, and my breath comes a little harder. How high are we going?

Hinges squeak on the floor above me. I focus on the stairs and cover the remaining ground until I reach the door the boy went through. A sign tells me I'm on the 29th floor. I lean my hands on my thighs for a moment and breathe deeply. Then I push the door open carefully, and step into a gloomy triangle-shaped space, in which I can just about make out the three lifts and five other doors.

A dark shape in the furthest corner detaches itself from the wall, and there's a light shining in my face. I blink and stumble away. My back hits a wall.

"Why are you following me?" He advances on me, holding a torch. The accent is pure East London.

"I'm not! I'm not!"

He moves so he's standing between me and the stairs. Does he have a weapon?

"Then why are you here?"

I take two quick breaths. *Think fast, Talia, and for goodness sake change your accent.* "I'm looking for my friend." I manage what I hope is a passable South London tone, rather than my usual BBC English.

"Which flat?"

"She ... she ... I don't know."

The boy steps over to the wall and flicks a switch. The landing fills with light and I flinch. I'm in danger if he recognizes me.

I cover my face with my hands, and make a sobbing noise. I'm not a good actress. But my face is already wet with rain. I rub my eyes, hoping my makeup is smearing all over my features.

The boy steps over and pulls my hands away from my face. I resist, but his grip is firm.

"Is that why you followed me?" he says. "You're lost?" His voice is kind, but patronizing, as if he's speaking to a simpleton.

I'm close to real tears now, and my voice breaks when I reply. "You ... you looked like you knew where you were going .... Out there, all the people ..."

"It can be hard, when you're first here. Let me guess. Evicted because of a minor conviction? A cold, or stomach flu, even though you're already better?"

I nod. He lets go of my hands. "It feels like the end of your life, I know. But you'll learn how to avoid the addicts and pickpockets. It's a strong community. We look out for each other."

I let myself look up into his eyes. The color of them still catches me by surprise.

"I'm Galen," he says, holding out his hand. Not Kieron, then. It's an odd name. Familiar, somehow. I offer my own hand and we shake. His grip is warm and dry.

"I'm ... Tanya."

"Tanya," he says, tilting his head. He noticed the pause. "Pick any name you like. It's a new start. Welcome to Shakespeare Tower. I can help you find your friend. I know most people around here. What's she called?"

Shakespeare Tower. Jack Benson said Shakespeare, didn't he?

For a moment I consider telling him who I'm really looking for. But I've been all over the television, all over the papers looking for Tig. I'm lucky he hasn't recognized me. He'll put it together if I ask about her. I try to come up with a common name, instead.

"Jessica."

He taps his fingers against his full lips. "One of the girls crammed into 8f is a Jessica, and there's a Jess in Cromwell Tower too. You can ask Johnny, he's the guy who sleeps in the foyer there, he's a good bloke."

"Thank you."

He waves a hand. "No trouble. We help each other around here." He pauses. "I hope to see more of you, Tanya."

In spite of myself, I feel my cheeks glow. It's not my fault. He is good-looking.

A creak makes him turn around. The door to 29e opens.

She's there: Tig, standing in the doorway.

She kicks at the door jamb. "What's going on? I heard talkin'." Her tone is surly, her accent even stronger than Galen's.

"Get back inside. What have I told you?" His voice is kind, but firm.

"Don' I get to meet your friend?" She's smiling at me. I swallow, trying to keep control as guilt and regret swell inside me for what I've done to her father.

"Tig …," Galen says.

Tig kicks the door jamb once more, then turns. She closes the door loudly, not quite a slam, but she's made her point.

Galen grins. "Sorry."

"Don't worry about it." My heart is pounding. I hope I still sound calm. "Your sister?"

His brow furrows. "My sister? What makes you think that?"

My mouth opens a couple of times. It was a stupid thing to say. She's much paler than him. I would never have said it if I hadn't known she's Jack's daughter.

"Dunno. The eyes, I guess."

"I'm babysitting. Her mum's at work." He's a good liar.

"That's nice of you."

He folds his arms. It's clearly time for me to leave.

"8f?" I ask.

"Yes, 8f. Or Cromwell Tower. Tell Johnny Galen says hi."

"Thanks so much." I'm backing toward the stairwell.

"No probs."

"See you around." I open the door, and slip through it, back into the stinking stairwell. I lean against the wall and breathe deeply.

I've found her.

I hurry down the stairs, careful not to trip. In the foyer, I peer out through the cracked glass before opening the door. The man with the blanket has disappeared, thank goodness. Instead of going through the central marketplace I head between the looming buildings, into the darkness of a narrow alleyway.

I've not gone far before the footsteps start. Behind me. "Hey, babe," comes a voice.

My muscles tense. I should have stuck with the marketplace. There's no one else here. I speed up. The thud of his footsteps gains pace too.

A wolf-whistle. I can't go back, but the path ahead is dark, deep in the shadows of the concrete high-rises.

"Why are you ignoring me, girlie?"

Keys jingle in his pocket, the noise louder as he gets closer. He's walking fast.

"Nice skirt, slut."

I break into a run.

The rhythm of his jangling keys picks up, echoing off the buildings. "Think you're too good for me, whore like you?" The footsteps speed up, shoes squeaking, getting nearer.

I push myself as fast as I can go, arms pumping as I strain forward. My breath is coming hard now. But there's light ahead, at the end of the alleyway.

Out-of-breath swearing, from too close behind me.

Then I'm on a raised walkway above a city street. There's a staircase down to a main road. I take the steps two at a time, hoping I won't stumble. The man behind me shouts, but his voice is getting fainter. I peer up and he's leaning over the walkway, mouth distorted as he screams obscenities down at me. I stumble onto Aldersgate, but keep running down the street, through the crowds, not stopping until I get to St. Martin Le Grand. I lean my hands on my thighs, waiting for my breath to come back, my heart to stop racing. I'm safe here.

A public telephone stands next to me. Perfect.

I can call social services with my South London accent, tell them where to find Tig, and head straight home.

CHAPTER EIGHT

PENTHOUSE FLAT,
BANKSIDE, LONDON
EIGHTEEN DAYS LEFT

AT HOME I THROW the clothes and shoes straight down the rubbish chute then fill a bath, pouring in every kind of lotion I have: lavender, vanilla, orchid, filling the room with perfume. I relax as I sink into it, close my eyes, and soak for a long time.

Tig will soon be pulled from that nightmare, soon be brought to a nice home, to warmth, love, plentiful food, and a world free from people begging, stealing, and grabbing at her. I've done good work today. I didn't fail her.

Why don't I feel better about this?

Perhaps because it's hard not to think about Galen. About his kindness to me, his green eyes. He doesn't belong there either. I try to push the thought from my mind. He's older than I am. He doesn't need saving.

The bath is getting cold. I should get out soon. I gaze around at my white, clean bathroom, starting to feel like myself again.

For a moment I wonder what it would be like to be Tanya, the girl I claimed I was, faced with the Barbican, knowing she has nowhere else to go. Is that fair? One crime and her landlord throws her out?

Thomas Bryce claimed it was unfair that he ended up there after

Dad brought him to justice. Said it ruined his life. But he was scum. Blamed all his problems on other people.

If Tanya had met Galen, he'd help her. If she were a decent person, she'd sort herself out. Get a job, be back on her feet in no time, and find somewhere else to live. I turn on the hot tap. There's no Galen in my life. No one ever offers to help me. Everyone assumes I'm doing great.

And I am, I remind myself as I lie back in the bath. I'm doing just fine.

※

I smile for my dad when they all come home the following lunchtime. He's tells me the press have called, that the girl from the hospital has been found and taken into care. The papers want a comment from me. Dad's overjoyed about it all. His poll numbers are way up, his lifelong ambition within his grasp, and the girl I was so worried about is safely in a children's home. It's a win all around, it really is. He swoops me up in a bear hug and I squeeze him back. He wouldn't be nearly as happy if he knew how she was found.

Piers approaches later, wincing as he puts weight on his bad leg. I'm eating delivery pizza in the kitchen. Alison and Dad are going over some notes for his next speech in the sitting room. I've been trying to ignore them, and the voices occasionally raised in laughter across the open-plan flat. I don't like the way Dad is smiling at Alison.

"You should visit the girl," Piers says.

"The girl? You mean from the hospital?"

Piers keeps his voice down. "The press are desperate for the follow-up on your heroics. It's a great story for us," he says. "The visuals are perfect: cute kid, teen saviour — the camera loves you. Apparently her mum is dead, and social services said she was staying with a dodgy guy."

Galen wasn't dodgy. I'm about to defend him when I remember I wasn't meant to be there.

"But we don't know anything about her. If she's happy about this or not."

Piers waves a hand dismissively. "Obviously we'd check out the situation before. I can send someone to do that. We don't want this to blow up in our faces in front of the cameras."

My heart beats faster. If he does that, he might find out about my visit to the Barbican.

"Better if I just go, without the press at first," I say quickly. "If I check it out before we bring the media in, we can be sure of how she'll react to seeing me."

When I get back, I'll tell him that it won't work, that she doesn't want to be interviewed, and I'll be in the clear.

"I'd usually send one of my guys. Just in case."

"I'll keep it quiet. And wouldn't that be a better story? That I've been visiting her in secret, not for the publicity. Before it's leaked, I mean?"

Piers taps a finger on his chin, thoughtfully. "I'll speak to your father. You have good instincts. I know you said you won't be the one to change the world, but we'll make a politician out of you yet."

Me, changing the world. I like the idea of that.

Piers continues. "I'd like you to speak at a fundraiser we have in a few days' time, and some rallies, if that's okay."

"And on the main campaign?"

"We'll see how these events go."

I grin at Piers. He can be hard on Dad, but it's only because he wants him to succeed. They're friends from back in law school, although Piers stuck at it, even after Dad left for politics. But after Piers was attacked, he gave up his practise and joined Dad's staff to advocate for other victims of crime who were denied justice. And he's loyal to Dad, not the National Law Party. If Dad loses, the party will get rid of him as soon as they can.

He's got as much riding on this as we do.

Piers heads into the sitting room, leans down and talks to Dad. I hear the low rumble of conversation. As I enter, Dad turns away from Piers and to me.

"This is what you want?" Dad asks.

I nod.

"I'm not sure, Talia. Some of those kids are pretty rough."

"They're kids, Malcolm," Piers says. "Relax."

"You have to let me do this."

Dad puts his arm around me. "You've been through so much, Talia. My little girl. You shouldn't have to deal with any of this."

"I'm not that little anymore, Dad."

"I suppose you're not." He sighs. "Well, have you still got mace?"

"Yes, Dad." I can't imagine using it on children, but I do have it.

"Bring that, then. Keep your distance from the kids. And have Mike drive you, and stay close to you."

"There's no need for worry," Piers says. "After what Talia did for the girl, I guarantee a warm welcome."

I press my lips together. I'm not so sure about that.

≠

The children's home is in Hackney, on Mare Street. We approach it along a street of shuttered businesses.

"Here we are," Mike says.

For a moment, I think he's got the wrong address, as we're outside a shop, complete with a green sign saying "Hackney Convenience." But then I notice a sheet of paper stuck in the window, with "Hackney Child Services" printed on it.

I take a deep breath and open the car door, letting the chilly air in.

"I'll circle around the block," Mike says. "Best not to park in this kind of neighborhood. Unless you need me to come in."

"I'll be fine, thanks."

I wrap my coat around me tightly as I cross the pavement. The door is unlocked, so I step inside and shut out the wind. But it's just as cold in here.

The room is about the size of a tennis court. Gaps show in the floor tiles where the grocery aisles used to be. Children of all ages mill about everywhere. An infant chews on an empty plastic bottle, teenagers congregate in a corner, and younger children run around, banging into each other, falling and crying.

There's a lump in my throat. I didn't think it would be like this.

It takes me a while to spot an adult. The nearest one is spooning some kind of mush to a baby in a plastic high chair. I'm almost knocked down on the way over to her by a gang of kids who sprint by.

"Hello," I say when I reach her.

She looks exhausted. She puts down the spoon, slowly.

I offer my hand. "Talia Hale."

"I know who you are." She wipes her hand on her jeans and shakes mine. "Jackie Musgrove. I wouldn't have thought our little facility was on the campaign trail."

"No, I've come to see someone."

"Of course. That girl from the hospital. Tigan."

I let my gaze wander around the room again. She obviously catches my expression.

"Not what you were expecting?"

I shake my head.

"The space was cheap to lease. We're on a tight budget."

"Where have all these children come from?"

"Some are orphans. Some have parents in Quarantine who might not come out alive. Some are only in our custody temporarily to stop them getting their parents' diseases."

She gestures to the room. "There's not enough of us. There's not enough money. Can you talk to your father about this?"

"Of course. He'll want to help. Will they be adopted?"

"A few will." She points at the infant she's feeding. "The youngest ones, mostly. No one wants them once they're over seven. They're ... well, difficult to control when they're older. And they're often in trouble with the law by then. No one wants to adopt a child who's under a Recall."

"How old's Tig?"

"Won't say. Nine, maybe? Won't talk to us. You might want to ask the boy who's with her. He's the only one she'll talk to."

I start at that. "Boy? What boy?"

She gives a tired shrug. "Some friend from the Barbican."

I scan across the room. Dread creeps through me. My gaze stops on a figure, his back to me. I recognize that confident stance, and he's turning around.

"I'll come back another time," I say too quickly. "I don't want to disturb her when she has another visitor."

Jackie looks as if she's about to speak, but I cut her off. "Thank you so much for your time. I'll tell Dad about all of this, don't you worry." Then I'm walking away, toward the glass door, avoiding the children as they careen around me, bouncing off each other like croquet balls.

I head outside, into the wind, without turning back. The car isn't there, and I hear the shop door open behind me.

"You!" I recognize Galen's voice and spin around. His green eyes blaze with anger. He shakes his head. "Tanya, Talia, you ...." He clenches his jaw. "Are you trying to destroy our lives?" It's clearly a real question, not a rhetorical one.

"I wanted to help." But it sounds weak.

"Well, you've really helped." His words are thick with sarcasm. "Taking Tig away from everyone who loves her and dumping her in a place like this."

"No child should have to grow up in the Barbican," I say, but my voice trembles.

"And yet hundreds do. You think this is better?" He waves a hand at the children's home.

"She might get adopted here," I say, in spite of what Jackie told me. "Might end up with a good family instead of the one she was born into."

Galen looks like he's been slapped. "And what's wrong with the family she was born into?"

"Her mother's dead, and her father is a dangerous criminal." I pause, the memory of Jack's face, pleading, coming back to me. "I'm sorry he's in such trouble though. I really am."

"Sorry? You hit him with a chair."

"I … I thought he was going to hurt Tig. I didn't mean to hurt him." I don't know why I'm trying to explain myself to this boy. It's his stare, like he can see right through me. "They told me he's a drug dealer, that he's violent."

I know I've said the wrong thing as soon as it comes out. Galen's nostrils flare; he's pulled himself up to his full height, and for a second I'm afraid. But he shakes his head.

"You saw a big black man and made assumptions. But he wasn't a drug dealer. He was a doctor."

My brow furrows. "What?"

"Well, he was a medical student. But he dropped out because he didn't want to just patch up injuries or transfer diseases. He believed in the Hippocratic Oath. He actually treated the sick; with aspirin, herbs, any medicines he could find or grow. Those were the drugs they're charging him with 'dealing.'"

My mouth opens and closes. I can't imagine the man I met in Quarantine doing any of that. I guess I did cause brain damage.

But that wasn't my fault. I thought he was going to kill Tig. What was I meant to do? How could I have known? Anger swells in me.

"So he tried to make criminals better? Illegally reduce their sentences?"

Galen's green eyes glisten. "He treated sick people! People whose only crime was trying to feed their families, trying to look after them when they were abandoned by society, used as a dumping ground for the diseases of the rich!"

I take a step back. "If he was such a great guy, what was he doing waving a cleaver around?"

"You don't understand!"

I put my hands on my hips. "Explain it to me, then."

He pokes a finger at me. "It's none of your business. You think you're entitled to know all about our lives, but you haven't got a clue what we've been through. I can't believe I tried to help you. I was so stupid."

"You tried to help me? I'm the one who went up against an armed man. I made Tig famous. Social services will find it easy to get a good home for her, a good family, now."

Galen snorts. "If social services could do that, I'd have taken her here myself. Can't you see why I wanted to keep her away from this?" He's staring hard at me, as though I'm an alien species he finds repellant, but doesn't understand.

"I'll tell my father about the homes. He'll sort this all out. Make them better."

He laughs. "Good luck with that."

"He will! He's a good man!"

"He's a rich man. They don't care what happens to us."

"Dad's not like that —." The sound of a slowing car comes from behind me. A door clicks open, and Mike is at my side, shoulders squared. "Do you need help?"

"No," I say. "It's fine."

Galen steps away from me, toward the children's home. "I should go inside. Tig needs me."

"Dad will make things better."

"Yeah, right." Galen opens the door, and goes inside. I watch him stride through the chaos toward Tig.

"Ready to go?" Mike asks.

I nod. Galen doesn't turn around, doesn't look back through the glass. Mike opens the car door for me and I slide into the back seat. There's a hollowness inside me. But I'll speak to Dad. He'll prove Galen wrong.

We'll fix this.

CHAPTER NINE

PENTHOUSE FLAT,
BANKSIDE, LONDON
SEVENTEEN DAYS LEFT

I WAIT AT THE flat for Dad to come home. This afternoon he's flitting from meeting to interview: a factory, a shopping center, and a school. After four-thirty is meant to be daddy-daughter time. But it's already five, so I message him. He says he'll be back soon.

It rains steadily, the water smearing down the windows, distorting the light in the apartment. I sit on the floor in the sitting room, thinking about the children's home, the Barbican, Galen, Tig, her father and all she's lost.

When the front door clicks open, I jump to my feet and run to Dad. I wrap my arms around him and the wet of his coat soaks through my shirt.

"Talia," he says. "What's this all about?"

"I'm pleased to see you," I say, my voice muffled against his chest.

He laughs, and pulls away. "At least let me take off my coat." He shrugs it off his shoulders, and water splatters onto the hardwood. Footsteps and conversation come from behind him, and the clack of a cane.

"Who's that?"

He avoids my gaze.

They're coming around the corner now. Piers and Alison. So much for daddy-daughter time.

"There was a crisis in Eastbourne," Dad explains. "Our candidate got caught drunk driving. It's too late to replace him, so we've got to figure out if we're going to back him or make him step down and throw our support behind an independent."

Piers nods on his way in. Alison tries to give me a hug, but I move to the side and apologize, as if I thought I was blocking her way.

"How did it go today?" Piers asks as he takes his coat off. "We could use a media distraction."

"Not good." I point toward the sofa. We file in together and sit down. I take the place next to Dad quickly, before Alison can get there. She slumps onto the armchair opposite.

Dad pats my knee. "I'm sorry to hear that, sweetie. Wasn't she pleased to see you?"

My gaze drops to the cream fabric of the couch. "Not exactly. There were so many children, so few adults, there weren't many toys, the place was ...." I'm searching for the right word. "Tatty," I say. I'm finding it hard to express what was so bad about it.

"For most of the kids, it's only temporary," Dad says. "Just while their parents are in Quarantine. And many of the others get adopted or go to foster homes."

"The woman there said people don't adopt the older kids. They find them too difficult."

Piers pulls out his laptop. "People don't want to take on teenagers with criminal records. But if they're good kids, there are homes for them."

"I'll ask around," Dad says. "Maybe I know someone who'll adopt the girl you saved."

I smile at that, and Dad puts an arm around me.

"But I promised the woman there that I'd talk to you about it, get you to help."

Alison leans forward from the armchair opposite. "And you have. You've kept your promise. You should be proud."

I ignore her. "Can't you do more, Dad?"

"We have limited resources. We'll do what we can, but not everyone can live like we do, honey."

"I'm not asking for them to have a place like this," I gesture around our huge flat. "Just somewhere nice."

"It's not just the money, Talia, although raising children is expensive. Ideally, we want them to stay with their families, right?"

"Well, yes ..."

"Parents want the best for their children. So if we spend too much, make the children's homes too nice, parents will abandon their children there. They'll think they'll have a better life there than they can give them. We don't want that, do we?"

I shake my head. Galen did say he'd have taken Tig to social services if he thought she'd be better off.

Piers is smiling. "This stuff is gold, though. You visiting the home, being appalled at the conditions. We can do a whole piece on how the current government let them slide, and how Sebastian Conway's party might make further cuts."

"I'd rather you didn't. That's not really ..."

"And maybe we can buy them some toys, some treats," Piers says. "Not from Government or party funds, of course. A personal donation, from you and your family. Don't you think they'd like that?"

"Well, yes, but ..."

Dad pats my knee. "It's a start though, isn't it? And when we win, we'll increase the funding if we can, okay?"

I look into Dad's eyes. There is concern there.

"They need more than a little increased funding."

"Go to Hamley's tomorrow," he says. "Pick out whatever you think they'd like. Take my credit card. And I'll speak to my advisors about longer-term solutions. Children are important. We'll find room in the budget."

I think of what Galen said, about hundreds of kids being raised in the Barbican.

"What about the others?"

Piers raises an eyebrow. "What others?"

"The children who don't go into care. The ones in the Barbican, for example."

Dad starts opening his briefcase. "We can't take away everyone's children, Talia. That's wrong."

"I'm not saying that. It's just that it's so horrible …." I stop myself. I'm not meant to have been there, after all. "I mean I've heard it's horrible. All smashed up, with people sleeping rough everywhere and using the corridors and stairways as loos."

Dad pulls out some notes, and starts skimming through them. "The Barbican is an architectural marvel. People like that are lucky to have housing provided." He spits out the word "people" and I know he's thinking of Thomas Bryce. "It's not our fault how they treat it."

Piers jumps in. "These are criminals we're talking about, Talia. We give them a place to live for free, and benefits. More than they deserve."

"If they're good people who made a mistake, they can get jobs," Dad says. "Get out of there, get a better life."

I don't know how to explain what I'm feeling. I want to talk about Galen, but I can't let them know I've been to the Barbican.

Dad laughs. "You know, you still scrunch up your face when you're thinking. You have done that since you were a small child. It's adorable."

I frown, wanting to be taken seriously. Alison is smiling indulgently, but Dad catches my expression.

"Okay, okay, I'll speak to my advisors about the Barbican too. We'll see what we can do to improve it when we're in power, make it safer for any children who live there."

I pause, trying to phrase the question I want to ask next. "Want to play interview?"

"We don't have time for this," Piers says.

"We'll make time," Dad growls at him.

"We have to talk about Eastbourne …"

But my hand is already in a fist, holding the invisible microphone in front of Dad.

"What would you say to those who claim we're using the poor as a dumping ground for the diseases of the rich?"

"That's propaganda," Piers says. "This isn't about rich or poor. It's about right and wrong."

"Quiet, Piers," Dad says. "This is my interview." He turns back to me, and his voice is soft when he speaks. "In the end, some people are going to be ill. It's not nice, and we don't want anyone to suffer. But we only sentence criminals to diseases. Isn't that better than having innocent people go through illness? Than having innocent children die?"

I don't know what to say, but Dad continues.

"That's why we have the justice system. That's why we have due process. So it isn't about rich and poor. It's about criminals and law-abiding citizens. And yes, criminals are more likely to be poor. Some people don't want to work. They'd rather steal, use drugs, or drink — sponge off the rest of us. And that's how they end up in places like the Barbican."

"Is that all better?" Alison's got this awful, deeply concerned expression on and I want to hit her. What does she care?

I shove the invisible microphone in her face. "What's going on with you and Malcolm Hale?" The question comes out before I think about it.

Alison freezes. I hear Dad's intake of breath from beside me, but I don't take my eyes off her. Her mouth opens and closes like a beached fish, and she looks to my dad for help.

"Talia," Dad starts. But I don't need to hear it. The answer is right there in the look that passed between them, in the pause before he spoke.

My hand is still clutched tight around my imaginary microphone, fingernails digging into the palm of my hand. "How long has this been going on?"

"A few months, Talia." Dad rubs at his forehead. "I didn't want you to find out like this. We were waiting for the right time to tell you. But we've been keeping it secret. It wouldn't play well in public because of the age difference."

Alison looks down at the floor and bites her lip.

"I am not the public." I run out of the sitting room and up to my room before he can say another word.

A couple of minutes later, Dad's footsteps thump up the stairs, followed by a knock on my door.

"Talia …"

I ignore him and throw myself on my bed. I'm being a total teenager, but I don't care.

"We should talk about this," he says.

A muffled voice comes from downstairs, calling Dad's name. It sounds like Piers.

"I'll be there in a minute," Dad replies, then he speaks in a quieter voice. "Talia, will you please let me in?"

I pick up my pillow, and put it over my head. Dad still paces outside.

"Malcolm!" That's Piers again.

"Please, Talia. We need to talk."

I don't say anything.

"We have to get on top of this before the six o'clock news!"

Dad takes a deep breath. "I have to deal with this Eastbourne situation, and if you don't want to talk right now, then we can find some time when you're calmer."

And with that, he's gone, footsteps retreating back down the stairs.

≠

The next day, Dad leaves for his flight to Edinburgh before I wake up. There's a note, saying he loves me and we'll talk later. He leaves his credit card on the kitchen table. Mike comes to pick me up after lunch, and drives me to Hamley's, where I run up Dad's bill as much as I can. He never set a limit, so that's his problem. Mike helps me carry the toys. It takes us three trips to the car to bring out my purchases: craft kits, puppets, costumes, remote control planes, paints, magic tricks, jigsaws, books, and science sets. We might not be able to fix the homes right away, but I'm going to try my best to cheer that place up, and Dad can pick up the damn tab.

I get back in the car, and we drive to Hackney. I wonder if Galen will be there this time. I think about him, and his green eyes — so much like Tig's. Maybe he is her brother. He's been visiting her every day, after all. I bet he lied about his name. Just goes to show that I can't trust a word he says.

I realize where I've heard his fake name before. Galen was an ancient doctor, like Hippocrates. And Galen told me at the children's home that Jack believed in the Hippocratic Oath. Perhaps that's where he got his street name, "Hippo." I guess that means Kieron's taken on his father's role, chosen an alias, and become a drug dealer too.

Part of me wants to show him all the toys we've got for the kids. But part of me dreads the judgment in his green eyes. My stomach churns as we drive past the shuttered shops.

When we reach the home, Mike helps me carry in the toys. The children swarm around us before I can stop them, and they're already carrying off the best ones, as many as they can, or fighting over who gets what. I look around for Tig. Jackie is walking over, shaking her head.

"What are you doing?" she asks.

"We brought some toys for the children," I say.

"I'm not blind." That exhausted expression clouds her face again. "You should have let me distribute them. Half of them will be broken by the end of the day. And some of them are choke hazards. The money would have been better used hiring some part-time help."

I pull a teddy bear out of the bag. I chose it especially for Tig. Rebecca had one like it. I look around.

Jackie inhales through her teeth. "No one bothered to tell you, did they?"

"Tell me what?"

Jackie's voice is expressionless. "That girl ran away."

My heart clenches. "Ran away? Tig? Where?"

She shrugs. "Child services checked the place she was living before, that boy's flat. She's not there."

I clutch the teddy bear tighter. "But she could be in trouble. We have to find her!"

Jackie raises a tired eyebrow. "How?"

I stare, trying to think of an answer. I have no idea where to start looking if she's not with Galen.

"Most of them turn up, sooner or later. We had some teenagers who ran away a few months ago. They were picked up by the police street-walking in Shoreditch, and they're back here now." She nods toward a sullen group of girls leaning against a wall, wearing short skirts and tank tops. One of them starts coughing.

Jackie must see the shock on my face, because she adds, "Don't worry. Tig's probably not become a prostitute."

My mouth falls open. I can't believe how casually she discusses this stuff. "Probably? She's ...." I'm about to say *she's only nine*, but that was Rebecca's age. We don't know how old Tig is. "She's too young," I finish, lamely.

"Fifteen is too young too. It's a bad world out there."

I glance over at the teenagers. They're younger than me? I thought they were way older. They dress like they are. One of them wipes her nose on her sleeve. She must have been sentenced to a cold. I feel the creep of guilt. But I had my cold transferred over a week ago, she couldn't have it. Whoever had it would be better by now, wouldn't they?

I reach for Jackie's arm. "There must be something we can do. For Tig, I mean."

Jackie gently pulls her elbow from my grasp, and there comes the defeated sigh again. It makes me want to slap her.

"There's not much we can do for her now. She'll have a criminal record whatever happens."

"She broke the law? What did she do?"

Jackie stares at me. "Running away from the custody of the state is a crime."

I blink. "A crime? Why?"

"Don't ask me. Ask your father. His party supported it."

CHAPTER TEN

THAT NIGHT I CAN'T sleep. The front door opens and closes at around midnight, but Dad's footsteps go straight to his room. Alone, at least. He probably doesn't want to wake me. And I don't want to talk to him right now. All my feelings about him and Alison and what I learned today mash up in my head until I'm rigid with anger. I want to ask him about the National Law Party's policy. I checked online and Jackie was right. The current government proposed the law on punishing children who run away from the state, and Dad's party supported it. Only Sebastian Conway's party voted against. How would Dad justify it?

I bet he'd say the law was for Tig's own good. To discourage her from running away.

But the law didn't stop her running away. And now she'll have a criminal record. No one will adopt her. And that's the least of her worries.

It's my fault. I put her in that awful home. If she's walking the streets, it's due to me. I should have left her with Galen.

But perhaps she's safe, hidden somewhere else. I doubt Galen would tell me, but if I see him, I'll know. As soon as I see his face

I'll know if he's as worried as I am, and perhaps I can help find her, help fix this. I'll be prepared, this time. I know what I'm going into. Dad and Alison wouldn't want me going back into the Barbican, but what do I care what they think?

I promised Jack. And, more importantly, I made this mess, and I have to put it right.

≠

As soon as Dad leaves the next day, I'm out the door. I shop smarter this time; go to second hand stores, buy an old hooded jacket with pockets in the inside lining, a stained T-shirt and jeans riddled with holes.

It's a sunny day, for a change, the light glaring down on the glass and steel of the city. I enter the Barbican by Aldersgate, the way I came out last time. Pulling my hood over my head so it half-hides my face, I slouch over, jam my hands into my jean pockets where I've hidden my mace, and try a "don't mess with me" walk. I feel silly, but there are fewer eyes on me now.

I make a beeline for Shakespeare Tower, avoiding the market. There are no hands held out for change as I walk by people huddled in their cardboard homes. I hold my breath as I pass. Most just glance at me with tired eyes. I peer out at the strange city. The arched windows at the top of the buildings, like raised eyebrows peering down on me. The confusion of walkways and ledges. The whole place looks like a filthy nightmare of an M.C. Escher drawing.

The entrance to Shakespeare Tower is in worse shape this time. Pieces of glass have fallen away from the shattered spider's web, leaving gaps in the window. They clink and grind underfoot as I step into the shadow of the building.

The bright sunshine makes it hard to see into the foyer. I stop inside the door to let my eyes adjust. There's the lift doors, the stairwell. Muttered voices come from the corner. Several shadows detach from the darkness and head for me. They're on me before I have time to react.

One shoves me, and I stumble back.

My hand flails for something to catch my weight against, and lands on the broken glass of the door. The edge cuts deeply into my palm, but the pain doesn't come yet. I struggle to regain my balance.

Time slows down. There are three of them, just shapes in the dark space. I judge where each of them is. Okay. I had self-defense classes. Dad insisted on them, after the attack. But why can't I remember any of that right now? My heart hammers in my chest. I duck to the right so there's one in front of me, his two friends behind him. They can't all get at me at once.

My eyes are adjusting. The first guy is about eighteen, hair shaved into a blue Mohawk.

"Your kind doesn't belong here. Get out," he says. But he's blocking the doorway.

Without thinking, I punch his face as hard as I can with my good hand. So hard I swear at the pain in my knuckles. But he barely moves. Just rubs at a slight red mark on his jaw.

I expected him to fall down. That's what they do in the movies — fall down when they're punched. I guess I'm not punching hard enough. But that was all my strength. What do I do now?

"What's the matter, princess? Break a nail?"

Mace. I have mace. I reach into my jacket pocket, fumble for the can, and pull it out, upside down. The guy with the Mohawk spots it. Takes a step back. I almost drop it from my shaking hands as I twist it upright, find the button on the top with my finger.

The guy on the left is nearer now, a barbed-wire tattoo crawling up his neck and over part of his face. I swing around to him and spray the mace in his eyes. He stumbles back, falls to the ground, screaming curse words and clawing at his face.

The third guy looks at his two friends. I hold the mace can toward him, trembling, and he backs away, raising his arms.

"Come on, let's get out of here," he says, and reaches for the guy on the ground. He pulls him to his feet and drags him out through the door. The boy with the blue Mohawk looks like he's going to come at me again, but I raise the mace and he backs off, joins the others.

That was easier than I thought. I guess Dad is right. He always says criminals are cowards.

Once they're gone I look at my hand, at the blood pooling on the floor. I swear, loudly. The pain is kicking in, no longer kept at bay by the adrenaline. It's a bad cut, deep and bleeding freely. Holding my palm to stem the flow, I try to think. There's no emergency department at St. Barts, it's just for Transfers. I don't know where the nearest one is. And even if I find an ER, how am I going to explain what I'm wearing and what's happened without the press getting wind of it?

I need a doctor, though. I glance at the stairs. Galen. I don't know for sure that he's taken on his father's role, or if he's willing to help, but I don't have any other options. I head for the stairs.

I barely notice the smell. I'm concentrating on climbing. I don't want to touch the walls, or the handrails, in case I get my cut infected.

I stop halfway up to cry. But I pull myself together quickly. This is no place to fall apart.

I'm dizzy when I reach the 29th floor, and I'm not sure if it's from the shock or the climb. I glance around the triangular space, looking for 29e, the one Tig popped her head out of. I stumble to it, and bang on it, hard, with my good hand. There's no peephole, I note with relief. Galen wouldn't open it if he saw it was me. I wait, then I bang again. What if he isn't in? Where would I go then? What if the thugs are back, waiting for me downstairs?

But it does open, on a chain. Green eyes peek through the gap. Galen recognizes my face, a flash of anger in his glare, but then his eyes travel down and he takes in the blood, all over my jeans and jacket, and still dripping from my hand.

The door slams for a second, but there's the sound of the chain being released. The door swings fully open, and Galen is standing there. I'm so pleased to see him, I smile. That surprises him more than my appearance.

His gaze falls to my bleeding hand. He curses under his breath. "What happened?"

"I got attacked … in the lobby," I pant.

His eyes widen. "The lads in the lobby did this? Bloody hell. You'd better come in. Quickly."

He steps out of the way, and I stumble into the flat.

"Follow me."

He leads me to the bathroom, all white with seventies fittings; so out of date they'd probably be fashionable again, if they weren't so shabby. Ancient grime darkens the grout. I hesitate before putting my hands near that sink, but the porcelain seems clean enough. Galen runs the cold tap, steers my hand under it. I flinch, and he studies my face. "Is that the only injury?"

I nod, not trusting myself to speak.

Galen grabs a fraying flannel from the side, and once he's rinsed the cut, he presses it to my palm, hard. I breathe in through my teeth.

"Hold that here. Come on," he says, and he leads me down the corridor, along the cream carpet. I try not to drip on it, but it's already stained and the flannel is quickly soaking through. We step into a small room with big windows. There's a kitchen in one corner and Galen heads for that, pointing at an old brown sofa.

"Sit," he says.

I do, pressing the flannel hard against the cut to try to stop the bleeding. I concentrate on breathing through my teeth to try to block out the hot pain radiating from my palm. The cloth is saturated, so I press the cleanest bit of the sleeve of my jacket against it, letting that soak up the blood. I hope whoever owned this thing before me wasn't sentenced to any blood diseases.

I watch Galen in the kitchen. He reaches for a first-aid kit, turns on the tap, and fills a bowl with water. He carries them both over to the sofa and kneels in front of me.

"Give me your hand," he says. I take away the sleeve, and he pulls my palm toward him. He cleans the cut again with the water, then pinches it open and peers in it. I close my eyes and breathe deeply through the pain. Fresh blood oozes out as he examines it.

His face scrunches up. "It's deep, but clean. You're lucky it missed the tendons. What cut you? Was it a knife?"

I shake my head. "Glass. They pushed me and I fell against the broken window."

He exhales, seems relieved. "That makes sense. How'd you get past them?" He opens the first-aid kit and picks a tube of antiseptic.

"I punched someone in the face," I say, trying to sound calm. "Got another one with mace."

Galen pauses, in the middle of squeezing a blob of cream onto his finger. "I'd never have guessed you'd outfight a bunch of Barbican lads."

"Well, I wouldn't say 'outfight' …"

"This is going to hurt," he says.

I try not to flinch, but he's right. As he smears the ointment pain stabs through my hand. My body goes rigid but I don't make a sound.

"You need stitches. You'd better get to a hospital."

I shake my head. "Are you any good at them?"

Galen raises an eyebrow. "Yes, but I don't have any local anaesthetic."

I can't go to a hospital, can't explain where I've been. "I can handle it."

Galen stands, walks over the kitchen again. He opens a sugar jar and pours the contents into a bowl. A box flows out with the sugar. He brings it over and I read the box quickly — "Surgical Sutures — single use — sterile." I wonder where he got those from. He looks at me, as if he anticipates the question.

"They're veterinary, but it'll be fine." He pulls a package out of the box and rips it open. There's a curved needle and some thread. He picks a pair of tweezers from the first-aid kit.

I breathe in sharply through my nose as the needle pierces the skin, and focus on counting under my breath as the pain shoots through my palm. Two stitches, three, four, five. But he's surprisingly quick. He ties the last one off, reaches for some small scissors, and trims the thread. He pulls a white roll of dressing from the box, and starts unwinding it.

My hand throbs, but it's bearable.

He gives me an appraising look as he wraps the dressing around my palm. "You'll need to remove the stitches in ten days, but you can do that yourself. You're braver than I thought."

"I've been shot in the head before. This is nothing."

"Of course." He finishes wrapping the bandage. "How much blood do you think you lost? This time, I mean."

"I won't need a transfusion, if that's what you're getting at."

He still crouches in front of me, holding my hand. I don't pull it away. His head is tilted to one side, and he's got that expression again, like I'm an alien, or some other creature he can't figure out.

"Why didn't you go to a hospital?"

"Didn't know where the nearest one was. Didn't want to explain this," I gesture at my blood-stained clothes.

"So your father doesn't know you're here?"

"No, but I've left notes in case I don't come back." It's a lie, but I don't want him to think I could disappear and no one would come looking for me.

He drops my hand, and I feel an odd disappointment.

"I just patched you up, and now you think I'm going to hurt you?"

I open my mouth to deny it, but his gaze stops my tongue. "Sorry," I say instead. "I … feel vulnerable here."

He stands up, paces to a bookcase. "So why did you come?"

"I'm looking for Tig. I need to know she's okay."

He turns around and I notice the mostly empty shelves behind him. I guess he's not able to afford books. "She's not here. The police searched already."

"I thought you'd know where she was ... Kieron."

The effect is immediate. His eyes widen. He tries to compensate, shrugs, presses his lips together. "I'm Galen."

"Galen was an ancient doctor. It's a pseudonym, like Hippocrates, isn't it? Your dad taught you, and you took on his role."

He holds himself rigidly. "I don't know what you're talking about."

I stand up, step toward him. "She's your sister. I just want to know that she's okay."

"So you can call child services on her again?"

I pause. I can hear a TV play in the next flat. The walls must be thin in this building.

"I didn't know about the homes," I say quietly.

"There's a lot you don't know. You should go."

The attack has taken the fight out of me. But he's clearly not worried about Tig. She's not here, but he must know where she is.

I back toward the hall. There's paper and a pen on a table by the door. I scrawl down my address and phone number.

"If you need anything, contact me."

Galen gets ahead of me, opens the front door. "Goodbye."

"I want to help," I say.

"You've helped enough. She'll have a criminal record now."

I hang my head, and step out of the flat.

Galen closes the door in my face.

I'm still for a moment, in the dark hallway, staring at the number on the door. 29e. Well, this was a waste of time. But she must be safe. Isn't that all I wanted to know?

I turn around and am about to head downstairs when I notice something.

I'm not even sure what it is, for a moment. I spin around on the spot. Three broken lifts on three sides of the triangular building. Five apartment doors. I heard the sound of a television, coming from behind me, when I was in Galen's flat, coming from behind this patch of wall. I can still hear it if I concentrate.

But there's no apartment door here.

What did Galen tell me, back when he thought I was Tanya? That there was a Jessica downstairs, in flat 8f. There's no flat f on this floor.

Two of the three walls have a lift and two doors each. On the third wall, there's a lift, 29e, and a blank wall where the sixth door should be. I walk over to it, knock gently on the wall. There's a slightly hollow sound, as if it's been plastered over. I think about the layout of Galen's flat, then I turn back to his door, and I knock again.

He opens it instantly. "What now?"

I push past him, stride back into the sitting room. I turn around, orientating myself to where I was standing out in the hallway, and listening for the television.

"What?" Galen says.

The bookcase. Of course. That's why he was standing in front of it when he was talking. I walk over.

"What're you doing?" His voice is rising, but he's still trying to seem cool.

There's no hinge, no secret mechanism, but most of the shelves are empty, making the bookcase light. I bend down and lift the corner, start to swing it away from the wall using my good hand.

"Stop that!" Galen says, but it's too late. Light comes through from the other side. I pivot it further, exposing the ragged hole knocked in the wall. There's a handle fixed onto the back of the bookcase, so it can be pulled into place from the other side. I step back, and look at him in triumph. He shakes his head, and I bend down and climb through the gap, and into the hidden flat.

What strikes me first is the green. There are plants everywhere.

Light streams through floor-to-ceiling windows at one side of the space. There are no walls, it's one huge room filled with plants, and a space cleared for a bed on the floor with a few toys next to it. There's the TV I heard, piles of books, and another old sofa. But the greenery makes it looks like a camp in the middle of a forest.

And sitting on the sofa is Tig.

CHAPTER ELEVEN

BARBICAN,
LONDON
FIFTEEN DAYS LEFT

GALEN STEPS INTO THE flat behind me, and Tig tilts her head to one side. She's got some threads in her lap.

"Kir?" she says.

Galen goes over, sits on the sofa and puts his arm around her. "It's okay, Tig." He turns to me, and there's fear in his eyes. "Right? You've seen the homes. You won't call child services again, right?"

I find myself shaking my head, dumbfounded. The space is beautiful, an oasis. I take it all in: the sunlight, the plants, the warm earthy smell of it all. Who would have believed the Barbican could hold such a paradise?

"I ... why would I take her away from this?" I gesture at the room. "It's wonderful." Galen smiles, with pride and relief.

"It was Dad's. He made this all, when he was well." He looks down.

"When he was well?"

"He was sentenced to measles just over a year ago. It's not usually serious, but he had complications — viral encephalitis — it messed up his brain. He almost died, and he wasn't the same after that. We took care of him, and he took care of the plants. It calmed him."

I inhale deeply. It wasn't me, then. He was like that before I hit him with the chair.

I've heard about severe complications of disease. It's rare, but Sebastian Conway says it's one of the reasons why we should vaccinate people, and give criminals medicine for the diseases they're sentenced to, instead of leaving them to suffer through it.

I stand still for a moment. I feel sick in this gorgeous garden, set in the sky above the Barbican.

"I thought he was going to hurt her," I say.

Galen holds Tig tightly. "I get that," he says. "And he was getting more violent, getting out more often. I was meeting a contact at the hospital, getting some supplies, and couldn't leave Tig alone with him, so I brought her." He kisses his sister on her head. "He knocked over the bookcase from this side. Got a cleaver from the kitchen, and followed us. When I saw him, I left Tig in the foyer. I thought she'd be safe there. I tried to talk him into going home, but he ran off. I don't know what was going on in his head."

Tig turns her face into her brother's chest, and he pats her on the back.

"I'm so sorry. If I'd have known ...."

Galen shrugs. "We lost the dad we knew a long time ago. And if you hadn't knocked him out, those bloody security guards or the cops would have murdered him."

Of course. It's shoot-to-kill at hospitals, after all.

I sink down to the floor, too overwhelmed to stand. "Why didn't you tell child services you're her brother?"

Galen wraps his arms tighter around Tig. "I'm only eighteen, and they think I'm a drug dealer. They'd never let me look after her. Probably wouldn't let me see her."

The two of them clutch each other on the couch, and I realize how unfair that is. How would I have felt if someone tried to separate Rebecca and I?

"She belongs here," I say.

Tig peeks out through her brother's arms. She gives me a little smile and I return it as warmth floods through me.

"What's in your lap?" I ask.

She holds up the threads; blue, white and black. "Friendship bracelet."

"It looks lovely. Is it for someone special?"

Tig nods, emphatically. "Someone who looks after me." She grins up at her brother.

I wave a hand around the room, at the plants. "How did your dad do all this? Create this space without people knowing?"

"Some floors only have four or five flats, so it looks normal to outsiders. Dad took on two flats, and knocked a hole through the wall." Galen gestures around the space. "Then Dad knocked down the other walls, and opened it all up for the plants."

"What plants are they?" I ask, although I already have an idea.

Galen pats his sister on the head. "Tig," he says, "Can you go to the bedroom for a mo?"

Tig gives us a funny look, but she jumps off the couch, taking the half-finished bracelet with her. She heads through the gap in the wall, and into the other flat. Galen stays seated on one side of the sofa, and I stay on the floor.

"You mean it?" he says. "You won't call the pigs?"

"No, I promise." I pause. "These are medicinal plants, aren't they, Kieron?"

He runs his hand over his hair. "Call me Galen, please. I prefer it. Some are food," he gestures to a corner, where tomatoes and courgettes grow. "We grow our own here. Benefits don't stretch far."

"But the others?"

Galen points at the plants on the other side of the room. "Sweet violet, mint, catnip, sage, quinine, and a load more. Not illegal to grow."

"But they're illegal to use."

"Sort of. Except as flavoring. Bit of a gray area."

I can't imagine any judge considering this a gray area.

Galen runs his tongue over his lips. "You lost your sister, didn't you? Wasn't she about Tig's age?"

"That's why I had to do something when I thought she was in danger. I did mean to help."

Galen picks at a loose thread on the armrest. "Can you tell me about …." He points to my head. "I mean, I saw it on the news at the time, everyone did. But things are different from how they are on TV."

I know what he's asking. He wants to hear the story of how I lost my sister and my mother. I hate talking about it, hate reliving that day. But I can't say no to Galen, not after ripping his family apart. And there's something about those green eyes that makes me want him to understand who I am, where I'm coming from.

"Dad was a lawyer before he was an MP," I say. "He prosecuted a lot of people. Thomas Bryce was just another criminal." He didn't look dangerous, either. Mid-forties, a little plump around the middle, clean shaven. And while Dad had become an MP by the time Thomas Bryce decided to take revenge on us, he was only a backbencher. It's not like we had security or anything. We didn't think we needed it.

Galen is listening, chin in his hands.

"Bryce worked in a bank until he was caught embezzling funds. Dad won the case, but Bryce blamed Dad for the severity of his sentence. He got tuberculosis. He said his life went to hell after that. After he ended up in the Barbican."

"So he came for your family."

I nod. "He said he was from the council and needed to check our basement. Had a fake ID. Mum let him in and left him to it. He must have been getting the gun ready. Psyching himself up. We were in the bathroom." My voice breaks.

Rebecca had begged Mum to teach her how to put on lipstick. We were sitting on the floor in a little circle. Rebecca smeared it when she tried to apply it, so she had clown lips, and we were all laughing.

"I didn't even see him. Didn't hear him come through my parents' bedroom. I heard a loud crack from my right and saw Mum jerk. Then she was slumping over, and blood was pooling on the floor."

And I just sat and stared at my mother, trying to work out why she'd stopped laughing, why she was bent over, in a puddle of red. Thomas Bryce was standing in the doorway, still in his workman's clothes, rage in his eyes. It didn't make sense.

Then I saw the gun hanging limp in his shaking hand. He was staring at Mum's body, like shooting her wasn't enough.

Normalcy bias. Those long seconds where you don't react. Where your brain can't make sense of your situation. I didn't have a chance to save Mum. But if I'd jumped to my feet the moment he shot her, I could have got between Rebecca and him. I could have grabbed the gun when it hung loosely from his hand and turned it on him.

But I didn't. I just sat there as he tightened his grip and raised the gun again.

"He shot Rebecca next. Right through the heart, they said. I didn't see it. I was looking at him. She was nine."

I've imagined it so many times, the bullet entering her little body, the shock and pain on her face, still smeared with lipstick. I was already on my feet, already running at him. Too late.

"I was trying to stop him, but I didn't move fast enough." My cheeks are wet. I wonder when I started crying. Galen's eyes are wide.

"I remember the handgun pointing at me, at my face, and then I was staring at the white tiles of a hospital ceiling." I lift up my hair a bit on the left side. Galen gets up from the couch, and comes closer. "Here," I take his hand, trace his fingers along the scar. "That's where the bullet hit. He must have thought he'd killed me too."

Galen's touch is gentle, and tears glisten in his eyes. He takes his hand away, slowly, and sits down next to me on the floor.

"He blew his own brains out after that. A neighbor heard the shots, called the police, so help was there quickly enough to save me. I should be glad Thomas Bryce didn't check me for a pulse."

I didn't feel glad in the weeks that followed.

"It wasn't like the movies when the person wakes up as good as new. There were operations. Months of agony. Months of physio, of speech therapy. I had to relearn a lot."

In the shapeless time that followed, I often wished I'd died there in the bathroom with my family. Or I wished Thomas Bryce was the one suffering. Wished I didn't have to lie in my bed through the long hospital nights, unable to sleep for pain, mentally replaying the attack, thinking of what I should have done differently. Even when I drifted off, I woke to the grief crashing in on me, fresh as if it had just happened.

"Dad spent most of that time in the hospital with me. He blamed himself for not protecting us — that's driven his career ever since. He wants to make sure people like that face justice, wants to prevent it happening to others. He wants to make the UK safer."

It's harder to speak now. Harder to shove the words out ahead of the tears I know are coming. "He was the only one who understood. Everyone else kept telling me how lucky I was to survive. My mother and my sister were murdered in front of me and everyone kept telling me how lucky I was."

I start sobbing, and hide my face in my hands, in the medicinal smell of the bandage on my palm. My back shakes and Galen wraps his arms around me, pulls me into the warmth of his chest, and holds me. I cry for my family, for myself. I let out the pain of my time in hospital, years ago, and the fear from the attack in the foyer. I lean into him, surrounded by his scent, earthy and fresh, like his flat. Finally, when the tears stop coming, I pull away gently.

He's looking at me differently now. Like I'm no longer the alien he can't work out.

"I guess you never know someone until you know their story."

He wipes at my tears with his sleeve, and smiles.

CHAPTER TWELVE

GALEN LETS ME USE his shower. It's clean enough, but the tiles are chipped, the paint peeling from the walls. I try not to touch anything, just in case. Galen lends me some of his old clothes. I tell him to keep mine. When I return home the doorman does a double-take.

"Costume party," I say as I head up to our flat.

When I get there, I pace around. I turn on the big gas fire and sit in front of it, watching the flames as they warm the room. It's good to be home. Good to be clean, and safe. I message Dad and he says he's looking forward to seeing me at the Justice Gala.

I'd forgotten that was tonight. It's a fundraiser for the National Law Party. As I pass the mirror by the front door, I catch sight of myself, and the state I'm in. I'd better rush if I'm going to be ready in time.

≠

Mike drives me to the gala. Dad is there to greet me as we pull up, flanked by Special Protection Officers. No Alison in sight, I notice with relief. I'm wearing a floor-length plum gown and my mother's jewelry. Elbow-length gloves cover the bandage on my palm.

Dad gives me a hug. "You look wonderful, as always." He takes my hands in his. I flinch, and he obviously feels the bulge of the dressing under the satin. He turns my left palm up.

"What's this?"

"Just a bandage. I cut my hand making a sandwich."

Dad sucks in air through his teeth in sympathy, gives me a hug and asks if I'm okay. Once he's established that it's not a mortal wound, we walk toward the entrance. The gala is at the Banqueting House on Whitehall, a gorgeous neo-classical building, all white rectangles and tall windows.

"There's something I want to tell you," Dad says.

He must see me frown, because he shakes his head. "Not about Alison. She's not coming tonight. We thought it would be best if she stays away for a bit. While you get used to things. And to let you and I have some more time together. But I've got some good news."

I don't say anything. I don't want to think about Alison, But I know he's trying to make things right.

"Give me five minutes when we get in to circulate, then I'll explain. I'm looking forward to hearing your speech."

I stare at him. "My what?"

Dad's brow furrows. "Piers said he'd talked to you about this. That you'd agreed to speak."

"That's tonight?" I've read the emails, of course. But I can't remember any of it right now.

Dad reads my terrified expression correctly, and pats the back of my hand reassuringly as we walk through the narrow doorway.

"It'll be fine. Piers will have notes for you. And this is a friendly crowd. They'd lap it up if you stood on a table and did the chicken dance."

We enter the main hall, with its soaring columns and chandeliers. People advance on my father from all sides. Soon he's lost in the crowd of friends, donors and other well-wishers, and we've been separated and swept up into a maelstrom of small talk.

I forgot to ask him about the law on children running away from the homes.

People congratulate me on my exploits at St. Barts. I'm hemmed in on all sides by strangers who want to touch me, talk to me, say they've met me. The buzz of the conversation is too loud, like a plague of insects filling the room. This is a bad place for Dad to try to tell me anything.

He's chatting to the Lord Mayor of London. I catch his eye and he winds up the conversation. They finish on a handshake. Dad grabs my arm and leads me off to the side before anyone else gets a chance to talk to him.

He leans in, right by my ear, so I can hear him over the chink of glasses and the laughter of the crowd. "I've spoken to my advisors about the Barbican, as promised."

He checks there's no one nearby. "Keep it under your hat, but as soon as we win, we're sending in the army; clean the whole place up, arrest anyone with an outstanding warrant or who's keeping weapons or drugs." He leans back. He looks proud, like he's brought me a present. "What do you think?"

I swallow. They'll find Tig. They'll find Galen's plants. He'll go to Quarantine, and she'll be back in the home, with a disease and a criminal record. I shake my head, I'm already trying to think of how to tell Dad to change his mind when I hear my name. I ignore it.

"Dad …," I say.

But there's my name again. It's Piers, and he's heading toward me as fast as his leg will allow. He grabs my arm. "I need you by the stage. Where have you been? I hope you've been practising your speech."

I was meant to be at home all day. What excuse do I have?

"Of course," I say.

Piers pulls me through the room to the side of the stage. He shoves some cards into my left hand. I flinch as they hit the stitches, but he doesn't notice.

"Quick recap, but it's simple enough," he says. "You'll be great! Good luck."

Then he's gone. I try to focus on the cards. The first one is straightforward: how much my father and I appreciate their support. The second one talks about the importance of justice, and fighting corruption in government.

Then there's a female voice, amplified, saying my name. I turn around. There's a woman on stage, her blond hair sprayed into a bouffant so stiff a hurricane wouldn't shift it. She's holding a microphone and staring straight at me. She beckons.

"Talia Hale, everyone; our hero, and soon to be Britain's First Daughter!" That gets a huge round of applause, but it makes me cringe. We're not America, we don't have first families.

Hands pat my back, encouraging me forward. What can I do? I head toward the stage, trying to get my thoughts under control, glancing at the third card. Something about vaccinations.

I pull my smile a notch higher and step onto the stage. I take the mic the woman offers and nod to acknowledge the applause until it calms down enough for me to speak.

I raise the microphone to my mouth. "Thank you," I say. "Thank you so much." There's another round of applause, thank goodness, because I have no idea what I'm going to say next.

I spy a TV camera in the audience. The news must be covering this gala. I wonder if Galen is watching, if Tig can see this on the TV in that beautiful green room. I stare out at the upturned faces, arrayed in the latest outfits from top designers, and I think of the cheap pink jacket and denim skirt, and how that stood out in the Barbican. What would they make of this crowd? All this money, when they have so little?

Galen would think we were the enemy. Planning to raid their homes, give them our diseases, and turn them out on the streets, then go back to our nice homes, congratulating ourselves on a job well done.

My mouth opens and closes like a goldfish.

The blond woman is still on the stage, clutching a microphone herself. She walks over, puts a hand on my shoulder, and I'm enveloped by her perfume, so floral I want to gag.

She turns to me, her blond locks as unmoving as a helmet, and raises the microphone to her lips. "So, Talia, we've all seen your exploits. Who'd have thought Malcolm's daughter would be such a crime-fighter herself!"

The crowd cheers, and I take a step back, but her arm prevents me going further. Would they still think I were a hero if they knew Jack's odd behavior was due to brain damage, and the girl I "saved" was his daughter? Probably. They'd think he deserved it. For dealing drugs.

The woman keeps me in her grasp. "And so modest, too!"

Her hand is like a clamp on my shoulder, she swivels me toward the TV camera. "Can you tell us a bit about the attack at the hospital? And how your father will deal with criminals, and keep us safe from incidents like that?"

My microphone is limp in my hand, so she shoves her own at my face.

"I don't think things are always as simple as they seem." I sound lame. The woman nods, clearly thinking I'm going somewhere with this.

"Good people make mistakes. Sometimes they end up in situations they don't deserve to be in."

The room is quiet, frozen faces staring at me. A door at the back opens, and two police officers come in, a man and a woman. I wonder what they're doing here. Maybe they're giving a speech later, too.

"Perhaps we could go a little easier on some people who commit minor crimes. Not write them off, but give them a real chance to be a part of society again."

I catch sight of Piers. His hand is over his mouth, eyes fixed on me. He gestures frantically at the cards I hold. Next to him is Dad, his brow furrowed.

"It's rare, but some of the complications of disease can ruin people's lives. That's not fair."

Dad starts walking toward the stage, the corners of his mouth turned down. The policemen are making their way through the crowd, too, from the other side. Two paths clear in the spectators, each leading their way to me.

"If we could take people's circumstances into account a little more …"

Dad's at the stage now, heading up the steps toward me. He steps onto the platform, beaming at the crowd. He puts his arm around me and takes the mic from my hand.

"What Talia is saying is that the National Law Party cares about everyone. We will make sure petty criminals have every opportunity to make their way back into society again, and the innocent are saved from both those who would victimize them, and the unpredictable nature of disease."

He gives me a gentle push, toward the edge of the stage. "Thank you, Talia." I head for the steps, my heels clacking, the scattered applause ringing in my ears.

The two police officers are there. I feel cold. What do they want?

Dad told me two policemen pulled him out of the Commons the day Mum and Rebecca were murdered. I look back at Dad, but he's thanking his supporters, smoothing things over.

I take the steps down to stand in front of the police. In my peripheral vision I see the TV camera tracking me.

The female officer steps forward. Her face is firm, no trace of friendliness or sympathy. She speaks quietly, and I have to lean in to catch the words.

"Talia Hale, I am arresting you for forgery and fraud. You do not have to say anything, however, it may harm your defense if you do not mention when questioned something which you later rely on in court."

CHAPTER THIRTEEN

BANQUETING HOUSE,
WHITEHALL, LONDON
FIFTEEN DAYS LEFT

I LEAN BACK, AS if I've been slapped. What's
going on? The policewoman continues with the caution. Around us,
the well-dressed party supporters move closer to catch her words.

"Anything you do say may be given in evidence." She takes a deep
breath. "It would be best for everyone if we don't have to use the
handcuffs."

There are flashbulbs going off around us, fast as strobe lighting.

She puts her hand on my shoulder, turns me toward the door,
and starts to guide me through the crowd. People are pushing to get
closer to us. People with cameras and microphones.

"There must have been a mistake."

The policewoman shakes her head, and we keep walking.

I twist my neck around. Dad's still on stage, mic in hand, staring.
"What's going on?" he demands, voice amplified.

"You can join us at the station, sir," the second officer, an older
man, says. Camera flashes focus on my father's baffled expression. As
I turn away, Piers is stumbling up the steps to the stage and leading
him off to one side, out of the glare of the media.

The police keep moving me forward. I hear the muffled sound

of the mic being dropped, and then we're out into the entrance hall. I don't ask if we can stop to get my coat, don't even think about it until we're outside and the wind is cold on my bare shoulders. I'm so exposed. There are more media here, TV cameras too, their lights blinding in the darkness outside. Someone must have tipped them off. I raise an arm to shield my eyes as shouted questions explode all around me.

The police car is waiting. The female officer opens the door, puts a hand on my head and guides me into the car, awkward in my heels and floor-length gown. I pull the last of the silky fabric in next to me, and she slams the door shut on the noise, the questions, the paparazzi outside. It's a relief when we pull away.

⟋

At the police station, they bring me to the custody sergeant, and take down my name and address. I'm in a daze as they stand me against a plain background and snap a photo: my mugshot. I hope the press don't get hold of it.

They show me through to a shabby interview room just as Piers arrives, still dressed in his tux. He takes off his jacket and his white shirt gleams in the too-bright fluorescent light. He tells me to stay silent so I sit there, shivering in my thin dress as a policeman presents the evidence.

They have the letter I forged on my father's paper. The CCTV showing me entering Quarantine. Frank's report on the "incident" with Jack. Apparently, they routinely check all permission letters with each MP's office. My father's secretary told them he hadn't written any in months. My father confirmed it, ignorant of my little outing.

Piers asks for a private conference with his "client." The police leave us alone in the room.

"Can I speak to Dad?" I ask.

Piers shakes his head. "I told him not to come down here. I had to fight him on that, but we don't want him photographed at the police station. He'll meet you at home."

I rest my forehead on the cracked surface of the table to hide my tears. I've gone from election asset to election torpedo in the space of an hour.

Have I destroyed my father's hopes? I'm such a bloody idiot. What will I be sentenced to? Mumps, perhaps? Maybe they'll give me a disfiguring illness, to make an example of me, or something dangerous, like polio. It won't be a venereal disease, at least. They don't give those to under-18s.

I might throw up.

Piers limps back and forth across the room like an injured lion in a cage.

"When I said you could change the world, I didn't mean this. Do you know what you've done?"

"Yes," I say without moving my head.

"Forging an official signature on Parliamentary letterhead! Going to Quarantine without permission! These are serious charges, Talia!"

I chew on my lip. I didn't consider forging Dad's signature a crime. It felt like faking a sick note for school: bad, but not criminal.

"Look at me when I'm talking to you, Talia!"

I do. His expression is fierce, and I wish I could look away again.

"This is a gift to bloody Sebastian Conway and the Government. I bet they used their contacts on the police force and made sure they got your arrest on film for maximum embarrassment." He pinches the bridge of his nose. "We have to manage this. You went there to speak to the man who attacked that girl at the hospital, right?"

I nod.

"Why? To gloat?"

"No! I thought he might know who the girl was."

Piers pauses in his pacing. "You were looking for her?"

"Yes. She acted as if she knew him."

Piers's face clears. His fingers drum on his smooth chin. "We can work with that angle. You'll get some sympathy. What did he tell you?"

"That he was her father. I found out later he had brain damage, that's why he acted that way."

The corner of Piers's mouth twitches. "Hmm. Best if people don't know that. Makes you look less heroic. We'll keep it simple. Stick with you trying to find the girl, and your dad was too busy to sign the form."

"But that's ..."

Piers holds up a hand to signal for me to stay silent. He starts pacing again as he talks, the clacking of his walking stick punctuating his speech.

"You knew he'd say yes, and you didn't want to bother him since he's so busy. You were just being considerate. I'll get him to agree that it was a misunderstanding."

"I don't want to lie."

Piers punches the table. "You already lied, Talia! You lied to all of us and got us into this! Let me write the script here." His fist is still clenched. "I'll clean up your mess, but you have to fall in line. The girl ended up in a children's home, right?"

"She ... well, she left. Escaped." My voice shakes a little. But I'm not going to tell Piers about Galen and the hidden flat.

"That's probably good. Don't want her going off script. Best if we keep the 'father with brain damage' stuff out of the papers."

My mouth falls open. How can he be so callous? He pulls up the chair opposite me.

"I need you on board, Talia. The election depends on this. You don't want to destroy your father's career, do you?"

My gaze falls to the stained table, my hands still in the elbow-length gloves. He continues.

"You won't need to say anything. I'll do the talking. We'll prepare a statement in which you'll confess to the crime and explain the mitigating circumstances. You plead guilty and, because we're not opposing it, our contacts in the judiciary can get this rushed through the courts."

Should I be agreeing to this? It's true, sort of. I did forge the letter to find Tig. I didn't mean any harm. And why should Dad suffer for my mistake?

Piers takes my silence as agreement. "We'll leak this story to the media, along with your apology, and we might be able to get you off with a stomach bug or strep throat."

⁓

Dad's not at home when I get there. It's late when we're done at the station, and Piers tells me he sent Dad back to the gala to smooth things over, then off to HQ for the debrief and phone interviews with key media to manage the situation I've created. Dad messages me that we'll work this all out, and that he loves me. But I don't hear him come in that night.

The next morning, he's not in the house. Did he stay with Alison? When the door opens at lunchtime, I run downstairs. I expect him to be angry, but the man standing in the doorway is exhausted. He doesn't take his coat off as he walks through to the sitting room and collapses on the sofa. Only then does he raise his eyes to me.

"Talia," he says, the disappointment heavy in his voice.

"I'm sorry." I've rehearsed better, of course. Gone through my defense, and how to explain my actions. But I was expecting anger, raised voices. Not this defeated version of my dad. I wonder if he slept at all.

He takes a deep breath in, rubs his hands over his face and beard. "Did they treat you okay at the station?"

"They … it was fine," I say.

"Good." He sits there. I wish he'd say something. Do something. Shout at me.

"I thought I could trust you, Talia."

"You can! It was just that one thing." But I'm lying again. There were those trips to the Barbican. But how can I tell him about that without betraying Galen and Tig? Perhaps he can hear the insincerity in my voice, because he drops his head into his hands.

"I can't cancel the campaign, and you can't come with me." His voice is muffled and I have to step forward to catch it.

I feel as if a light has been extinguished in my chest.

"What?"

Dad lifts his head. "I wanted you to come with us on the road. I don't want to be without you for that long. But the media will hound you if you're there. And you need time to recover from whatever they sentence you to. You can get serious complications with diseases. I can't risk your health. You're too important to me."

"But I …"

"No buts. You'll stay in the flat while I'm away, and I'll get Alison to check in on you, and she'll stay here once you're no longer contagious."

"No," I say. The anger rising in me comes as a surprise. "I am not being babysat by your … your … whatever she is!"

"She's my girlfriend."

I put my hands on my hips. "I'm not the only one who has been hiding something. You should have told me! You shouldn't have …"

"Yes, I should have told you. I am sorry. But we're serious." He shakes his head. "I want you to get to know her."

"I already know her as well as I want to."

Dad rubs at his eyes. "I could have sent someone else to Quarantine to ask about the girl. You didn't need to lie to me. You talk to me, if something's on your mind."

"I've been trying, Dad." There are a lot of things on my mind. Alison, right now. And the image of the two of them together. I wish

I could block it out. "I tried to talk to you about the homes. And about the Barbican. But you wouldn't listen."

"I did listen. I set up the raid."

"You have to call that off."

That jolts Dad out of his exhaustion. "What?"

"It's not good for the people there."

Dad's brow is furrowed. "It will be good for the law-abiding citizens, for the children. Clean out the scum. Leave it safer for them."

I flinch when he says "scum." "But some people only committed minor crimes."

"Then they'll get minor sentences. They'll be okay."

"Some people haven't had a fair shot." I stare at my hands in my lap.

"The judges will take mitigating circumstances into account." Dad shakes his head. "I don't get this. Why have you changed your mind?"

What can I say? How can I explain why my opinion has changed?

"Is this because you're going to be sentenced?" He sighs, puts a hand on my shoulder. "No one there committed crimes for reasons like yours. Yes, you lied to me, but you did it out of concern for the girl. You're a good girl. A caring girl."

"There has to be another way. Please, Dad."

"I've told our cabinet. There's full support. I can't cancel for no reason."

He doesn't get it.

"What is this really about, Talia? What aren't you telling me?"

"Nothing," I say, but my gaze must give me away.

"What are you keeping from me? Do you have more secrets I should know about?"

I could ask him the same question. But I pause for too long.

"What else have you done?" He swallows. "Have you put yourself in more danger? Have you broken other laws?"

"No," I say, answering his second question. But I'm not even certain about that. I know where a fugitive is hiding. Am I an accessory?

Dad stands up. "You're keeping things from me. Defending criminals. I don't know what's happened, but I'll be honest. It feels like you're betraying the memory of Rebecca and your mother."

That makes my head hurt. "I'm betraying Mum's memory? You're the one sleeping with Alison. How would Mum feel about that? No wonder you're hiding it from the voters."

"Talia!"

"Look at yourself, Dad, lecturing me on keeping secrets, when you say you're serious about that cow, but you're keeping it secret because of politics?"

"Don't call Alison that."

"I don't want to hear about Alison. I don't want to hear you defending her, or hear how great she is, or see her wearing the same clothes two days running because you've been screwing her in our home!"

He looks like I've slapped him.

"She wouldn't be with you if you were anyone else, you know. You're too old. She just wants to be the prime minister's wife. She doesn't care about you!"

Dad's mouth is a straight line. "Go to your room."

"Why? Do you have yet another important political meeting I'm getting in the way of? Or are you heading off to sleep with her again?"

He doesn't say anything to that, just breathes in hard through his nose. And I don't want to look at him anymore. I turn and storm off up the stairs. He doesn't follow me.

≢

I avoid Dad for the next few days. It's not hard, since he's never at home. He leaves me messages, but I don't reply.

Piers works to fast-track my case, and since I'm pleading guilty, we're in court a few days later. With Transfer waiting times growing daily, it's easy to justify the expedited sentencing. The room is packed with spectators, and the media. I don't have to say a word. It's good, because I'm scared. There are no guarantees that I'm going to get off lightly.

I've been told to shut up, sit still, and look contrite as Piers speaks on my behalf.

He picked out my outfit. I hate it, and struggle not to fiddle with the tight Peter Pan collar. He obviously decided to make me look as young as possible. I'm surprised he didn't put my hair in bunches.

Dad sits next to me. He pats my hand during the hearing, and kisses my forehead. But I wonder if it's for the court's benefit, not mine. He's sitting too stiffly, his whole body turned slightly away from me, toward the judge.

Piers is good. Even I almost believe him. But as the case goes on I get more worried. The judge peers over his glasses at me several times and I try to look apologetic. Maximum sentencing for forgery is tuberculosis. And painful and disfiguring diseases are common. I've heard shingles is awful. You can end up with permanent scars, or blind in an eye. And what if I get a Recall? I'll spend a year wondering if there will be a pandemic.

But the judge addresses me when he's announcing his decision. Uses phrases like *irreproachable character*, *heroic actions*, *mistake*, and *concern for others*. I'm getting away with a slap on the wrist. Piers is beaming already.

It's the flu, in the end. No Recall. Backs are slapped, and I'm led outside to face the press. Piers has kept my speech short, and has told me to stick to the cards we wrote together. I'm in no mood to disobey.

"I'm sorry," I say into the microphones. I picture two pairs of green eyes, the people I should be apologizing to. "I accept full responsibility for my actions, and the consequences. If I could go back and do things differently, I would."

Then I'm led away, and into the criminal section of the Old Bailey, to cross the bridge to St. Barts for the sentence to be carried out.

CHAPTER FOURTEEN

St. Barts Hospital,
London
Eleven Days Left

THEY CALL IT THE Walk of Shame. It was added onto the Old Bailey in the seventies. It's a glass-walled passageway that leads over Newgate Street and straight into the back of St. Barts. Not the nice, new building where I first encountered Jack, but the brutal concrete block where convicts receive their diseases.

The media are in the street below, with long-lens cameras, waiting to get a snap of me. I keep my eyes forward as I'm led out of the Old Bailey and onto the passageway. Take care to look contrite, but unafraid. My ballet flats make a smacking sound against the floor. I keep my chin up and walk straight on. From the corner of my eye I can see them, crowded on the street below on both sides, flash-bulbs sparkling in their midst like glitter. The more enterprising have got into the buildings on either side, and white light pulses from open windows. It's only about twenty paces until I'm across, but it feels like much longer. I never thought I'd see this place from the inside. The older court officer presses a button to open the brown double doors and I'm led into St. Barts.

The antiseptic smell reminds me of my stay in hospital after the shooting. Of grief, pain and anger. The floor covering is wearing through in the middle of the corridor, and the concrete shows in patches. The walls are covered in linoleum too, but it's peeling away where it meets the ceiling.

Someone is screaming in a room halfway down the corridor. I know the Transfer hurts when you're receiving, but I didn't know it was that bad. I thought that was just what they put on TV for more drama.

The younger court officer seems to read my mind. "Don't worry, you're just getting the flu. Not like him, poor sod."

We get closer to the door, and the screams get louder. I won't cover my ears. I won't. I grind my teeth as we pass. The screams pursue us down the corridor. Now it sounds more like an animal in there than a human in pain.

My each step is reluctant now, my body locked with fear. My knees don't want to bend, and my arms are poker-straight at my sides. The younger court officer puts his hand on my shoulder and pushes me on.

We keep walking, to the fifth door on our right. Then the court officer places my folder in the file rack on the door, and opens it.

There are no sheets on the bed, but leather straps lie across it, with ankle and wrist cuffs at the sides. I stop in the doorway and stare. It's just like on crime shows.

"Do you have to strap me down?" I say to the younger court officer, but it's the older one who answers.

"It's policy. Never know what criminals are going to do."

The younger court officer flinches when his colleague says "criminals." He pats me on the shoulder. "There can be some involuntary movement, and with needles in your arms, you might hurt yourself."

Involuntary movement. I don't like the sound of that. I take two deep breaths. Whatever happens, I have to maintain my dignity. One of these men might sell my story to the tabloids.

"Lie down," the older man says, pulling the straps out of my way.

I want to run, but how would that look? Malcolm Hale's daughter, trying to escape justice? So I lie down on the bed. The older officer slaps the leather strap across my chest, and quickly buckles it. The other man gives me a grim smile. He has dimples on each of his freckled cheeks. He can't be much older than twenty. "Sorry about this," he says.

The older man pulls the straps tight. His mouth is hidden by a gray beard and mustache, but I can tell by his eyes that he isn't smiling. The younger man doesn't tighten the straps as hard, and it leaves me feeling lopsided.

I turn my head to the side, and there's the receiving Transfer machine. It has more buttons, pipes and wires than the one on the other side. Next to the bed, in a metal medical bowl, are three large needles, still in their sterile packs.

The younger officer follows my gaze. "There's more work to do on this side of the Transfer," he explains. "If you're transferring a disease out of a sick person, the immune system is working with you. But if you're the recipient, the body recognizes the virus cells as alien when your blood pumps back from the machine into your body. It tries to reject them. That's why it's more ... uncomfortable."

I know that. But I don't like the way he says uncomfortable.

The older man starts fiddling with the needles, opening the packages. He pulls up my sleeve, and the younger man does the same on the other side. I turn to the ceiling, and focus on the discolored concrete, the exposed pipes, the streaks of rust.

The sharp pain of a needle in my upper arm makes me flinch. Then there's another in my left arm. The older man moves down to my hand, and I close my eyes as the third needle goes in. I'm breathing fast now, but at least the needles are done. There's tugging and movement on them as they're hooked up to the tubes, and then the cold of electrodes attached to the skin of each arm. I focus on the blackness behind my eyelids.

The Transfer machine hums as it is turned on, and pain jars through my system. My eyes fly open.

The younger man is leaning over me, his face sympathetic. "It's always a bit of a shock at first."

The older man gives an odd laugh. His colleague glares at him.

"I thought you were making a joke," he explains. "Shock: you know, because of the electricity."

I don't find it funny. It's not as bad now it's constant. But it's a lot more than uncomfortable. It's a burning under my skin, nothing like the comforting tingle of the other side of the Transfer.

I try to breathe deeper. In. Out. In. Out. I slow my breath down. I can do this. I've been through pain before. This is nothing.

But then the older man hits another switch on the machine and the tubes fill with red. My blood. And there's a new pain. A sucking, pulling ache, like it's draining my strength, dragging at my veins.

I'm not even breathing. I'm trying not to make a noise. This is just for the flu?

I'm too hot. My head and heart are pounding.

"Try to relax," the younger man says. "It won't hurt as much."

Relax? Is he joking? My body is rigid with the searing, tearing pain that aches through my arteries and under my skin. I can't hold my breath any longer, and now I'm gulping like a fish out of water, my breathing out of control.

Couldn't they give me painkillers? Anaesthetic?

Burning, through my veins.

I remember. They used to give anaesthetic. But the Government changed the law years ago. Dad's party supported it.

My back arches, pushing my chest up.

Dad said we were going easy on thugs and murderers. Wasting taxpayer money.

I jerk and the older man pushes down on my shoulder, holds me in place.

I agreed with Dad. I never imagined this happening to me. I thought criminals were exaggerating how much this hurt. That they were weak, as well as cowards.

When will it stop? How long has it been?

I imagined killers like Thomas Bryce here. People who didn't deserve anaesthetic.

Everything is agony, my body one block of pain.

They do this to children too?

Breathe in and out. Don't scream.

But I deserve this for getting Tig a criminal record.

Stay still. Don't scream.

I deserve this, for not fighting the Transfer of diseases to children.

My blood is on fire. Don't scream.

I deserve this, for supporting the ban on anaesthetic.

I squeeze my eyes shut. The pain is red against my lids.

Don't scream.

CHAPTER FIFTEEN

MIKE IS WAITING OUTSIDE, wearing a face mask even though he's put the glass up between me and him. He drives me home without a word. The second I step out and into the building he pulls away with a screech.

I'm still shaky as I walk through the foyer. Twenty minutes is nothing when you're on the other side of the Transfer, but in the criminal wing pain pulled time and stretched it out.

I have to stop, and lean against the wall for a moment. The doorman doesn't make eye contact as I head into the lift. I slump down on the floor and listen to the pounding of my pulse in my head as I speed upward. I drag myself to my room and collapse on the bed.

I wake too hot, my clothes soaked in sweat. It's evening, as the room is dim. I sit up, but the movement sends pain crashing through my head. My duvet is on the floor. I must have kicked it off in my sleep. My nose is wet, snot running down my face and blocking my breathing. I wipe it with my hand. Gross, it's green. I sniff, but it doesn't help and for a second I'm disgusted by the noise alone. I sound like one of them. A criminal.

This is what brought down the current government. In the end, it wasn't the corruption, it wasn't even the convictions for embezzling public funds. It was the long-lens shots of the Prime Minister's face covered in chicken pox, the Chancellor of the Exchequer wiping snot on his sleeve. Even after they recovered, no one could respect them. But they stayed in power right until the bitter end of their term, knowing they'd lose the next election.

I squeeze my eyes shut to block out the stabbing pain in them. If the flu is such a mild illness, what must the others be like?

I have to message Dad. It probably won't work, but what else can I do? I don't want Tig to have to go through this. The bright light of my phone's screen makes me blink. I tap out a message.

"I need to talk to you. When will I see you?"

It's five minutes before the reply comes in.

"Not for a few days. I'll call when I can."

I type, "We need to discuss the raid."

I sit in the semi-darkness, staring at the screen, as my head pounds. There's a longer pause this time before my phone buzzes.

"I'm not discussing policy with you."

I sit there, feeling the sting of that reply. But another message buzzes in right after. It says, "Get well soon. I love you."

I hold the phone against my chest.

Thirst scrapes at my throat so I stumble into the bathroom to get a glass of water, and wipe this stuff off my face. I pick up the loo roll and lean against the wall, trembling. I'm already out of breath, my airways clogged and swollen. A cough forces its way up, and then my whole body is shaking with the force of it, racking through me.

I can't stop. I'm going to suffocate.

But it subsides, eventually. I lean my head against the wall. I can't prevent the raid right now. I'll try again tomorrow.

⚜

Halfway through the next morning the loo roll is finished, the floor littered with disgusting crusty green tissues, my bin overflowing. Dad cancelled the maid service for the week, partly to prevent me infecting anyone else, and I'm sure, partly for fear of photos being taken and sold to the tabloids. They've replaced my bedding with cheap sheets, so it can all be burned once I'm better. They're scratchy, not like my usual Egyptian cotton.

I wonder whose disease I've taken. Are they grateful that I'm going through it, and not them? I doubt it. It never occurred to me to be grateful to the criminals who took my viruses.

As soon as my headache allows, I watch the news on the television in my bedroom. Dad is still in the lead — just. Piers pulled out all the stops, called all his contacts to spin this our way, and it's working. A talking head on the BBC claims I was caught on a technicality, that it was a witch hunt perpetrated by a hypocritical and corrupt government, and that pleading guilty shows how honorable I am.

That makes me feel like even more of a fraud.

I drift in and out of sleep as the day goes by. The click of the front door unlocking wakes me, mid-afternoon, and hope bubbles up in my chest.

"Dad?" I croak.

"Talia!" His voice. His deep, wonderful voice.

"Dad!"

Then his footsteps come, heavy on the stairs. He opens the door a crack and peers through. There's a mask over his nose and mouth, but his eyes are crinkled in a smile.

He picks his way between the crumpled tissues, carrying a paper bag, as I pull myself up in bed.

"I didn't think I'd see you for days! Was there a cancellation?"

Dad shakes his head.

"You pulled out of a function for me?" I feel the tears coming, but I swallow, and force them back down. "I'm surprised Piers let you do that."

Dad gives a short laugh. "Piers isn't happy with me right now, to put it mildly. But some things are more important." He puts the paper bag on the ground, and sits down on the bed next to me. I throw my arms around him without thinking, then let go and back away.

"Sorry. Sorry. Can't risk making you sick."

But Dad leans forward and hugs me close. "I should have been there to pick you up after the Transfer. I should have stood up to Piers earlier."

My face is against his jacket, and I'm worried I'm leaving snail trails of snot on the soft black pinstripes. I pull away, slightly. Dad lets his arms drop, limp at his sides. I guess he took that as a rebuke, not an attempt to save his suit from the mess that is my face.

"I'm just glad you're here now," I say.

"I can't stay for long, I'm afraid. But I wanted to bring you this." He picks up the paper bag, and pulls out a large Styrofoam take-away cup. "Chicken soup. I heard it's good if you're ill."

I haven't eaten in over a day, and it smells amazing. "Thanks, Dad. You're the best."

"And you can order anything you like from the delivery menus in the kitchen drawer. I'm leaving my credit card here. I just need you to rest and take care of yourself. Okay?"

I nod, trying not to salivate at the salty smell of the chicken soup. But there's something I have to say.

"Dad, please call off the raid on the Barbican."

He stiffens. "Talia, I told you I wouldn't talk to you about policy anymore."

"But …"

"I don't understand. You were the one who wanted to sort out the Barbican. And I know how you feel about that place, because of …"

He's about to say "Thomas Bryce." But he stops. "I just don't understand, that's all."

"Things aren't how I thought they were. Things …." I don't

know how to explain it; my head hurts. I'm too tired and the words catch in my throat, bringing on another fit of coughing. Dad pats my back.

"Let's just leave it, Talia. I have advisors. Experts. People who have spent their whole lives looking at these problems. And I can't reverse all that based on the whims of a sixteen-year-old who can't even explain why she's changed her mind."

"Is that how you see me?" I say, once I can speak again. "Just some idiot teenager?"

Dad sighs, drops his head into his hands. "No, Talia. You're normally a very rational girl. But you've been through a lot these past few weeks. And I haven't been there as much as I should have been."

His phone starts buzzing. He glances at it.

"I'm sorry, but I really do have to go." He stands, bending down to give me one more hug. "I love you. And Alison will be around to look after you in a couple of days. Rest up, and get well. I'll see you in 10 Downing Street. I'll have more time then."

"No, please ...." But my voice is weak, and he's already standing.

"I wish I could stay." He looks away, but I'm sure I saw tears. "But I've missed so much to come here already."

I want to argue. Want to stop him going out that door. But I know how much it must have cost him to come here. To hug me, and risk needing a Transfer.

"I love you, Dad," I say as he gets to the door. He turns, and I can see that smile over his mask again.

"Love you too."

"But ... the Barbican ..."

He steps out and closes the door behind him, softly.

≠

The doorbell rings the next morning. I yank a dressing gown over my pajamas and struggle downstairs. I reach the door and peer through the spyglass. I make out the distorted image of the doorman, his face rounded by the lens.

I undo the latches and click the door open. I start coughing. The doorman takes a step back. He holds a bunch of flowers up in front of him, as if they're a shield.

"These came for you," he says.

I take them. They look familiar — the bright purples, the deep oranges. There's a card nestled in the middle of the blooms.

"Who sent these?"

The doorman shrugs. "Delivery boy didn't say anything. Wasn't even wearing a uniform." He's already backing toward the lift

"Thanks," I say.

He jabs at the buttons. The doors close as I turn around and step back into the flat, locking the latches carefully behind me.

Are they from Dad? I fish for the card, pull it out, and discover it's not a card at all, it's a piece of paper folded into quarters with a handmade bracelet wrapped around it. I head for the sitting room and slump down on the sofa. I lay the flowers next to me and unfold the paper. It says:

Talia,
Being sick for the first time sucks. Get better soon. My sister made you this friendship bracelet to cheer you up.
G.

Tears come to my eyes. The band that has been tight around my heart for the last few days loosens, just a notch.

I put the bracelet on and admire it. It's made with pink, purple, and blue threads. I try to smell the flowers but my nose is too blocked up. They're beautiful, their colors so bright in this sterile flat. I'll have to find a vase for them. Galen and Tig must have picked them for me, and Galen went to all the trouble of bringing them here. I feel warm.

Then the band tightens across my chest again. The army will storm into the flat, ripping down the bookcase and destroying the plants, the beautiful oasis. They'll strap Tig's small body to a bed at St. Barts and watch her screaming as they transfer a disease into her veins. They'll shove her back into the chaos of the children's home, sick and far away from the brother who loves her. Galen will end up in Quarantine, as doomed as his father.

I have to warn them.

CHAPTER SIXTEEN

IT'S TWO DAYS BEFORE I'm even a little better. But I have to go to the Barbican now. Alison said she'll work from our house once I'm no longer contagious, so she can keep a closer eye on me.

Dad clearly doesn't trust me at all. And he's probably right not to.

I shower and dig out the clothes Galen lent me when I was last there, then plaster on some makeup. The girl who stares at me from the mirror looks nothing like the me I'm used to. There are dark bags under my eyes and my skin's gray.

I stuff a wad of loo roll into my pocket. As soon as I step out of the flat I realize how weak I am. I lean against the wall of the lift on the way down.

The walk across Southwark Bridge is the toughest part. The wind is high, and I barely keep my balance as it tries to push me off the pavement into the traffic. It seems farther to the Barbican, hauling my feet along while my whole body aches. I wipe my nose as I pass a man sleeping in a cardboard box. For a moment all I want is a box of my own so I can curl up and rest for a while. The normal people I pass move out of my way, disgust on their faces. Some cross the road, others practically tightrope-walk on the curb to be as far away from the sick girl as possible.

This time, when I enter the Barbican, coughing, no one gives me a second glance. My disease makes me blend in. People still don't want to get close, but at least here they don't look at me like I'm something they've scraped off their shoe. I even get a couple of sympathetic smiles as I stumble through the gray labyrinth. A black woman with neat cornrows pauses as I pass and reaches into her bag. I tense, but she pulls out a tissue and offers it to me. I fight back the tears as I thank her.

I know my way to Galen's place now. I glide through the crowds like I belong here.

I pause outside Shakespeare Tower. The glass has gone completely and the foyer is empty. Above, two neighbors chat over their balconies, their laughter floating down to me.

I head inside, and pull the stairwell door open. The climb up to Galen's flat nearly kills me. I have to stop at the top of each flight as I'm coughing too hard. I sit down, picking the cleanest bit of floor I can find.

But eventually I make it to the 29th floor. I knock on the door and no sound comes from inside. I hope Galen isn't out and I've wasted a journey.

I knock again, the sound echoing through my aching head, and this time I do hear a noise.

When he opens the door, I practically fall into his arms.

"Talia," he says, reaching out to steady me. "Are you okay?"

I try to reply, but all that comes out is a hacking cough.

"You've come for medicine?" Galen asks.

I shake my head as he leads me into the sitting room of the first flat. He gestures to the couch and I collapse on it.

"What is it, Talia?"

More coughs wrack through me.

"Rest. Get your breath back. I'll put on the kettle." He heads into the kitchen.

"Thanks," I croak, as soon as my coughing subsides. "And thanks for the flowers. They ... they meant a lot to me. "

While he's filling the kettle, he looks back up at me. "You shouldn't be out. They won't treat any complications you end up with."

I don't reply. My voice isn't strong enough to carry to the kitchen. I wait until he returns.

"I had to warn you while I had the chance." My voice breaks as he heads across the room. "My father is planning ... a raid on the Barbican, with the army, as soon as he's PM."

Galen freezes, mid-step. His eyes move to the bookcase. "Do you think they'd find ..."

He doesn't need to finish the sentence. "They're planning to search for drugs and weapons. Every inch." I'm getting my breath back, but my words are fainter. I shouldn't be using my voice this much.

Eyes still focused on the bookcase, Galen combs his fingers through his short hair.

"You need to get out. Stay somewhere else," I croak.

He shakes his head slowly. "We have nowhere to go. You've no idea what this means. There are loads of us. Loads of people they call 'illegal' in here. We'd all be screwed."

"I've tried to talk to Dad. He won't change his mind."

"This place is all we have. They've taken everything else. They can't have this. No."

"I could take out some of my savings. Pay for a hotel for a few weeks."

"And what, be homeless after that? I need to speak to some people. We can't let them do this."

"You can't! You can't tell anyone!"

Galen turns to me. "You knew it would ruin our lives, and you couldn't let that happen to your friends, right?"

I nod.

"How can I let that happen to my friends? My neighbors?"

My head pounds. "You can't tell the … others here," I say.

Galen raises an eyebrow. "The criminals, you mean? Like you, me, and Tig?"

I shake my head. "I got attacked here … remember? You said there were no-hopers and addicts here yourself when we first met."

"When you lied so you could steal my sister away from me?"

"I was trying to help." It takes effort to make myself heard.

"And you thought I was a no-hoper then too, right?"

"I … you seemed helpful."

Galen throws his hands up. "That's how it is to you, right? The good guys and the bad guys. Splitting the world in two, like a bloody film."

"No …," I say, but he cuts me off.

"You'd have been happy getting us out of here and leaving all the other families to go through hell."

I want to say something, but he's right. I hadn't thought beyond warning Tig and Galen.

"I thought you were okay, Talia, but you don't understand anything. You'd better leave. You shouldn't be out of bed."

"I …"

He shakes his head. "Get a taxi home. Rest."

What can I do? I want to argue with him, want to tell him what I went through to get here. But I have no voice left, and I'm exhausted. I stand up, still feeling weak, and head out of the flat. Galen shuts the door behind me.

Have I made a big mistake?

PENTHOUSE FLAT,
BANKSIDE, LONDON
SEVEN DAYS LEFT

MY TRIP OUT DOESN'T take too much of a toll on my recovery. But I spend a lot of the next two days sleeping. It's easier now. My nose isn't running so much, and when I cough it's not unstoppable. Alison moves in on the third day.

It's hard to avoid her. I hate seeing her in my home, hate how she's already treating it like her own, leaving dirty dishes in the sink. She keeps checking in on me, always asking if I need anything. She works in the dining room, constantly on the phone, and there's nowhere on the main floor where I can get some privacy. But I'm not going to be chased out of my own sitting room. So I ignore her, even when she brings food, and puts it in front of me. Or asks me how I am.

Her phone buzzes constantly. So when it does for the millionth time, I don't even notice until she swears.

"I see. Have we put out a statement yet?" Another pause. "Okay. And which channel?"

To my horror, she comes into the sitting room, phone pressed to her ear.

"Sorry, Talia," she says, and she reaches for the remote control.

She stops my film and switches over. "Okay, yes. Of course. I'll make sure I'm caught up." She hangs up, sits on the couch and points at the news onscreen.

"Something's going on at the Barbican."

I jolt up in my seat. "What?"

"Let's see."

It's hard to tell what's happening at first. There's text scrolling below an image. Something about barricades. The camera is zooming in on London Wall, the entrance to the Barbican I used the first time I went there. It's pouring with rain and the passageway has been blocked with furniture, boxes, bags of rubbish.

"… lawlessness." The voice of the newsreader says. "Reports have been coming in of roaming gangs, breaking into flats, committing brutal assaults and burglaries. Can you tell us any more, Andrew?"

A reporter is cowering under an umbrella and trying to talk to people on the other side of the barricade. A black guy with a barbed wire tattoo up his neck is sitting astride a table at the very top.

It's one of the thugs who attacked me in the foyer of Shakespeare Tower.

"If it's a war they want, we'll give them one! Bring it on, pigs!"

He beats on his chest and whoops.

I stare at the screen. "What's going on?"

"Piers thinks they know about the raid." Alison points at the guy. "The criminals have barricaded themselves in."

My stomach clenches. "Does … does Piers know how they found out?"

"Didn't ask him. But there are a lot of people involved in the planning." Her brow furrows. "Talia, did you tell someone about the raid?" She sounds as if she is speaking to a child.

I ignore her, and focus on the screen. The camera zooms in on the guy who attacked me as he carries on ranting in the rain. "We'll defend this place to the death!"

"Talia?"

He's holding up a broken bottle, and the camera focuses on it. Something catches my eye. Something on his wrist. A handmade black, white, and blue friendship bracelet.

The anchor said that gangs are breaking into flats. Attacking people, robbing them.

I feel sick.

"Talia, do you know anything about this?"

Tig made that. I'd recognize it anywhere. Did he hurt them when he broke in? Did he steal it from Galen's wrist?

"Talia! Answer me!"

I stand up. The vision of Galen and Tig, lying in a pool of blood, like Mum and Rebecca, sears through my mind. This is my fault. The barricades. The attacks.

I thought I was some kind of a savior to her. To them. But I've ruined their lives.

In a trance, I head out of the room.

"Where are you going, Talia?"

"Upstairs," I say.

"Come back here. We need to discuss this. Did you tell someone about the raid?"

I pause. The stairs are to my right, the front door ahead of me. On impulse, I swing the door open, and run outside. I slam it behind me. Thank goodness the lift is right here. I run into it and hit the door-close button.

"Talia!" A muffled shout comes through the front door, followed by the click of the latches. But the lift doors are already closing and I start descending.

CHAPTER EIGHTEEN

SOUTHWARK BRIDGE,
LONDON
FOUR DAYS LEFT

SECONDS LATER, I'M OUT on the street. I'm not wearing a coat. The rain soaks through my red jumper, sticking the wet fabric to my skin. The water runs off my hair, down my face, and over my arms, clutched tightly around me.

Alison can't be far behind. I dash down the stairs at the side of Southwark Bridge and into the pedestrian tunnel underneath. At least there's some shelter from the rain here and she won't know which way I've gone.

As soon as I'm in the tunnel, I lean my hands on my knees, coughing. I've been so stupid.

Yes, Galen and Tig could be hurt, or worse. They'll need help, and the police aren't getting into the Barbican. But I shouldn't have acted on impulse. I should have planned my escape, put on a disguise. Brought mace, and possibly a weapon. But if I go home now, I'll never have another chance to get to the Barbican. Alison won't let me out of her sight after this.

Stupid, stupid, stupid.

I'd better get moving, in case she looks here. I head through the tunnel, and out the other side, into the rain falling on the banks of the Thames. It's not far to the Barbican, even this way. I can cross at London Bridge and double back along London Wall.

But it takes me longer than I'd thought, and my phone buzzes in my pocket several times on the way. The first three times, the caller display says "Alison." The fourth time, it reads "Dad."

I am in so much trouble.

I'm weak, and by the time I reach London Wall, I still don't have a plan. I lean against the side of a building, and ignore the stares as I wipe at my nose and struggle to stop coughing. It's getting dark.

Above me, through the rain, loom the towers of the Barbican.

I peer down London Wall. The flashing lights of police cars illuminate high barricades of junk. Media vans and reporters huddle on the other side of the road, filming from under umbrellas. But there are walkways that run into the Barbican all around here. I take a few steps and peer down Fore Street. Only two people guard the nearest barricade.

That makes sense. The narrow walkways and steep stairs here only allow single file entry. And the steps are overlooked on all sides by the estate. It would be a deathtrap for police trying to fight their way into the Barbican.

But maybe a single person could talk their way in.

I head down Fore Street, coughing. A heap of furniture and rubbish bags blocks the bottom of the nearest stairs, with another at the top. Two teenage girls are sitting on the walls above the entrance, ragged umbrellas over their heads. The sound of their laughter reaches me over the constant drumming of the rain.

"Hey," I shout, shielding my eyes from the water pouring down. "Can I come in?"

One of them leans over, bleached blond hair swinging from a wet ponytail. "You want to come in? Why?"

"I need to speak to Galen. Do you know him?"

The purple-haired girl examines me for a long time. Her gaze goes down to my soaking clothes and back up. I cough a bit more, deliberately this time.

The blonde smiles. "You know Galen?"

"He's a friend." Well, the closest thing I have to a friend right now, anyway.

The purple-haired girl is still staring. "Only the pigs want to get in here."

The blonde laughs. "Yeah, she's a one-girl SWAT team. Stop being so paranoid, Kaylee. Come on up, then."

My shoulders relax. Thank goodness.

I grab on to a chair sticking out of the barricade at eye level and find footholds among the rubbish. I heave myself up, over the wet furniture, table legs jabbing me in the stomach. I pause to cough on the other side before climbing the steps, then struggle over the second barricade and into the fortress the Barbican has become.

I wipe the water from my face as I orient myself and look through the confusing mess of buildings for the middle of the three big towers: Shakespeare Tower.

"Thanks," I say to the girls as I pass.

The purple-haired girl tilts her head. "Do I know you? You look familiar."

My stomach clenches. "Probably from around." I try to keep my voice light. "See ya!" Then I dash off before she has a chance to work out why she recognizes me.

It's eerily quiet in the city in the city, and getting dark. The only people are clustered around the barricades. There are small fires lit in barrels here and there, and the sound of music carries, even though the rain. A woman with a guitar is lit by the flickering flames of the nearest fire, mouth open in song. It feels peaceful on this side. Friendly even, compared to what the news was reporting.

But it was dangerous how close I came to being identified, stupid to come here at all. What was I thinking? I keep my head down, and

I soon wend my way under the buildings and along the walkways to Shakespeare Tower.

The foyer is empty, but I creep to the stairwell, and drag myself up the stairs. My shoes squelch, and I try not to cough. I don't want to attract attention.

I'm catching my breath on the 28th floor when a door opens above. There's footsteps, and laughter. I lean out and see a blue Mohawk.

I freeze.

It's the guy who attacked me in the lobby. I duck through the nearest door, and into the hallway of the 28th floor. I pull the door almost closed behind me and peer through the gap as he comes down the stairs.

He's followed by the guy with the neck tattoo, still wearing Tig's bracelet, and the third one who I fought off that day. My heart drums on my ribcage. Why are they there? To finish the job? Am I too late?

The second they've gone by, I slip out of the door and up the last flight of stairs. I burst into the hallway on the 29th floor and hammer on the door. There's a footfall in the corridor, then Galen's voice.

"Guys, what did you forget this time?" When he opens the door, there's a grin on his face. It fades into confusion as he sees me, dripping wet.

"You know those men?" I say, gasping for breath.

"Are you okay?" he asks. "Where's your coat? How did you get in? What are you doing here?"

"What were *they* doing here?" I demand. "Those are the thugs who attacked me!"

Galen grabs my arm and pulls me inside. He checks the hallway and shuts the door behind me. "I'll get a towel."

I push through and walk to the sitting room, where I start pacing as he heads into the bathroom, comes back with a towel, and holds it out. I ignore it.

"They're your friends?" I feel like he's punched me in the gut.

"Yeah," he says. "But it's not what you think."

"I saw one of them wearing Tig's bracelet on the news, and I thought he'd stolen it. I thought you'd been hurt, or killed!"

"She gave it to Reece. He and Gazzer are like brothers to her. Look after her a lot when I'm out helping people."

My mouth opens and closes. "But they attacked me!"

He takes a deep breath. "You weren't meant to get hurt."

I'm shivering. I just stare at him.

He turns away. "After Tig escaped from the home, I thought you might come back, or send someone. So I asked the guys to keep an eye out. Scare off anyone who didn't belong." He looks me in the eye. "No one was meant to get hurt."

I hold up my palm, show him the scar. "Well, in case your memory is fuzzy on that, I did."

Galen shrugs. "I was protecting Tig. Keeping her out of that bloody home."

A wash of guilt sweeps over me.

"Did you ...." I take a deep breath. "Did you do this? Did you tell people to start the barricades?"

Galen slumps down on the sofa. "I didn't know it would end up like this."

"So all of this is your fault."

"I guess."

I shouldn't have trusted him. I launch myself toward him. I'm slapping and scratching and he's batting away my hands. He grabs hold of my wrists and stops me. I'm panting, shaking with anger. Another cough wracks through me.

He lets go and I step back.

"We have a right to defend ourselves," he says. "But it got out of hand."

"Out of hand? You know there's going to be a war, right?" I breathe in fast. "You've made them more determined to send the army in."

Galen hangs his head.

"That's it. This is your problem. I'm leaving."

I head for the door.

"You can't leave," Galen says.

I turn to him. His chin is thrust out and his eyes hard. I keep backing toward the door. Galen follows me. I'm about to run when he speaks again.

"It's not safe out there. Not in the dark. Not for Malcolm Hale's daughter. Do you have any idea what they'd do to you?"

"I'd rather take my chances out there than in here."

Galen shakes his head. "I can't let you."

"I didn't ask for your permission." I get the door open, but Galen is at my side in a flash, so close I feel the warmth of his body. He slams it closed.

"Don't be an idiot, Talia," he says.

I yank at the door. "I can look after myself. Why do you care, anyway?"

His muscles tense through his T-shirt. He's strong. I can't even open it a crack.

"Because everyone in the Barbican will be punished if the future prime minister's daughter is murdered or raped here tonight."

I look up and into his green eyes. I think of the dark towers, the hidden corners. He might have a point. I keep pulling on the door though. I don't know what else to do.

There's a sneeze inside the flat. Galen's shoulders slump. He lets go of the door and heads back to the sitting room. I follow far enough to see that the bookcase has been pushed away from the wall a few inches. A little face is peering through the gap. It sniffs.

"Tig's caught a cold," Galen says. "So I guess I'm stuck looking after two children tonight."

"Did I give it to her?" I say. "When I came over sick the other day?"

"Maybe." I follow him into the flat as he keeps talking. "But lots of illnesses do the rounds here. We've better immunity than you, and we can't get them transferred without getting arrested. So we put up with them."

He opens the bookcase enough for Tig to enter the sitting room. She takes a few wary steps in, watching me the whole time.

"Tig," he says. "Talia will be staying with us tonight."

"Is she your girlfriend now?" Tig asks with a cheeky look.

My face heats up.

"No!" Galen says, the word coming out with a weird laugh that's almost a cough. "She can't go through the estate at night. I'll be taking her out first thing in the morning."

I nod. "First thing."

Tig sneezes again, into her sleeve. But she's still grinning. A ten-year-old is better at handling an illness than I am.

"Go to bed," Galen says. "I'll bring you a honey and lemon in a minute." His voice is soft.

"And read me a story?"

"And read you a story."

Tig disappears through the gap in the bookcase and Galen turns to me.

"Take the damn towel." He holds it out. "You can sleep on the sofa. I'll get you some dry clothes and bring you a blanket."

I take the towel, sit down, and dab at my wet hair. The towel is so thin it barely helps.

"Do you have a phone? Shouldn't you call someone?" he asks.

"I … guess I should call Dad. I ran out on his girlfriend when I thought you and Tig had been attacked."

"You did what?"

"I panicked. I … thought you might need help."

Galen's expression softens and he joins me on the couch. "And you came all the way here, in the rain, while you're still sick?"

"Stupid. I know. I didn't take anything with me. No money, no coat."

He pats me on the back. "So you're a penniless criminal stuck in the Barbican?"

I can't help but laugh. But it's a bitter laugh.

"I guess I am."

"Then you came to the right place. But you're going to have to call your dad and come up with an excuse. He can't know you're in the Barbican. We'll get you out of here tomorrow, okay?"

"Thanks."

"It sounds like you could use a honey and lemon too. It'll make you feel better. Trust me."

And in spite of everything, I do.

BARBICAN,
LONDON
FOUR DAYS LEFT

GALEN WHISTLES WHEN I pull out my phone. "Whoa, keep that thing under wraps. People in here would kill for that. Literally."

I peer at my phone. It's last year's model. I've never been an up-to-date gadget kind of girl.

"I should go and check on Tig," Galen says, and gives me a wink as he climbs through the wall. He must know I want a little privacy for this.

I click on Dad's name in my phone's contact list. This conversation isn't going to go well. I pace the sitting room as I wait for the call to connect, trying not to notice the holes in the carpet, the peeling wallpaper.

It's answered at the first ring.

"Talia," Dad says. "Where are you?"

"I'm safe."

"That's not what I asked. What the bloody hell are you playing at?"

"I had to do something. Don't worry. I'll be home tomorrow."

"No you won't. You'll be home tonight."

I keep pacing, but don't speak.

"What is all of this about? Is this because you're angry about Alison?"

"No, Dad. It's everything. I've learned a lot these last couple of weeks. I … don't know what to believe anymore."

"What do you mean?" Dad sounds impatient.

"About the Transfer, about the laws, about people who aren't as lucky as we are." I turn and pace back the other way.

"This is emotional blackmail. Go home now. My policies aren't going to be dictated by a teenager acting up over my girlfriend."

"I said this wasn't about that!"

"I can't see how this could be about anything else! Piers said he let something slip before your interview on *Sharpe*, and you started behaving strangely right after that." There's a deep breath from the other end of the line. "Look, I should have told you about Alison. I am sorry for that. But we are serious, and …"

I tune my father out. There is no way I'll convince him that I mean what I say without explaining everything. And I can't do that without giving away Tig and Galen, and telling him where I am now.

I interrupt him. "My battery's almost dead, Dad." That's not a lie, at least. "I'm safe and I'll be home tomorrow. Don't panic, okay?"

I hang up and turn the phone off before he can reply.

≠

A pounding on the door.

I wake and stare around, unable to distinguish between my dreams of distant shouts and screams, and the reality around me. The cluttered room is utterly alien, bathed in the gray pre-dawn light. There's a twinge in my back from the weird angle I've been sleeping at. I sit up and a blanket slides off me: brown with a diamond pattern. I remember Galen handing it to me last night.

He comes down the passageway wearing nothing but his boxers. I try not to stare.

"All right, all right, I'm coming," he says to the door. Then he hisses at me, "Get behind the bookcase. Now." I roll off the couch and climb through the hole. I reach for the handle on the back, but before I can pull Galen shoves the bookcase back in place.

I listen at the gap. The room behind me is still dark, and Tig snuffles in her sleep. Galen's footsteps cross the room outside and there's the sound of the door opening.

"Ben, what is it? What's happened?" Galen's talking but he's muffled.

"It's Sophie, in 3c," a gruff voice says. "She's been attacked."

"Give me a second to get my clothes on." The clunk of the door being closed. A moment later, the bookcase moves and Galen's face peers through the opening.

"What's going on?" I whisper, stepping out into the main flat.

"Duty calls. Can you look after Tig for a bit?"

I only pause for a second. I didn't tell Dad what time I'd be home, at least.

"Of course. How long will you be?"

"Dunno. But thanks." He dashes down the hall and comes back wearing jeans and a shirt and carrying a bag.

"We'll get you out of here soon, I promise," he says before he runs out of the door.

When he's gone I take a quick shower. They only have a sliver of soap, so I don't use it. I try to dry myself off on the fraying towels, but they feel like they spread the wet around. I miss the power shower back home, my fluffy towels and array of body washes and gels. I pull back on the clothes I slept in, feeling as if I hadn't washed at all.

I'm not sure if Tig is expecting someone to get her up or not, so I sit close to the bookcase in case she calls out. But it's still early. The sun is rising. I stand at the window. The rays have reached Galen's flat and are slowly, reluctantly, working their way toward the ground.

They reveal a mess.

In the tent village below tarpaulins flap in the breeze and cardboard boxes lie crushed on the ground. People are huddled together in one corner of the courtyard, individual homes abandoned.

I didn't notice any of that last night. What happened out there?

There's a noise from the other side of the bookcase, so I step through. The greenness of the room still surprises me, the morning light shining through the leaves, brightening the bare concrete walls and floor.

Tig groans and rolls over. She flops onto her back, then opens her eyes.

I smile. "How are you?"

She isn't surprised to see me. She sits up, raises a hand to her forehead, and flinches.

"You have a headache?"

"An' a throat-ache an' a eye-ache an' a bellyache." She starts coughing, folding up in the middle, her whole body shaking. I pat her on the back, feeling useless.

"Galen's gone out," I say.

"He's out a lot," Tig replies, when she recovers. "He's got loadsa people to help."

"And he's asked me to take care of you. So what can I get you for breakfast?"

She starts coughing again. That sets me off, too. When we're both done, she looks up. "I'm not hungry."

She's so fragile, so small. Smaller than Rebecca ever was. Her collarbones jut out through her skin.

"How about a honey and lemon, then?"

She peers up at me from under her eyebrows. "With double honey?"

"Triple."

I'm glad I paid attention when Galen was making our drinks last night, so I'm able to prepare it okay. I want a cup of tea, but all the mugs are chipped and stained. So I get a glass of water instead, and join Tig in her room. There's something I have to say to her.

Something I've been wanting to say, even though I know my words will fall laughably short.

"I'm sorry. About your dad, I mean. I didn't know. I thought he was going to hurt you."

Tig is watching me over the rim of her mug. Her green eyes never leave my face.

"S'all right. He wasn't my dad. Not really, not after the brain disease. My dad was smart and kind." She lowers her drink, rests it on her leg. "I was scared of him at the hospital," she says in a small voice. "I miss him, though. The dad we used to have."

"I'm still sorry. And about the children's home too."

"Galen said you were jus' a bit stupid about stuff."

I can't help but laugh. "He's right. I was a bit stupid about a lot of stuff."

I spend most of the day in Tig's room, waiting for Galen to come back. Tig is getting worse, coughing and sleeping more as the day goes on. I sit on the cold concrete, waiting for Galen and wondering what we're all going to do.

When Tig wakes in the afternoon we watch the news together. The camera pans over queues outside St. Barts. Criminals from all over London are hiding out in the Barbican, so there aren't enough recipients for the Transfer. They've declared an All-Level Recall to deal with the problem, and the hospital is handing out antibiotics as a stopgap measure. People's tempers are fraying. They're blaming the nurses, the police, the Government, and, most of all, the people holed up in the Barbican.

Sebastian Conway and the Democratic Justice Party are trying to negotiate. Offering an amnesty if the barricades come down. But no one wants to talk with politicians who look like they're going to lose next week. My father's pulling ahead. When the anchor has finished going through the poll numbers, a realization shoots through me.

I don't want Dad to win.

I want the amnesty. I want negotiation. I want things to be better here, in the Barbican.

They cut to Dad giving a speech, calling for emergency measures, martial law, and there's an ache in my chest. He looks so tired. I'm betraying him by being here, by wanting him to lose. But I still wonder if he misses me. If he still loves me. If he'll ever forgive me. I wipe away the tears before Tig can see them.

Then the anchor comes back on. I'm not really listening, until she says something about a deadline, and a raid. Then I sit up.

The news cuts to the Prime Minister, at a podium spiked with dozens of microphones.

"We can't wait until the election. These criminals cannot be allowed to have a stronghold in central London. They're defying a Recall. If they do not dismantle the barricades, then we will be forced to tear them down and drag them out from their hiding places, kicking and screaming."

I swallow. Of course the Prime Minister is threatening a raid of his own. It's a vote winner, and the Government is desperate to be seen as hard on crime.

"They have thirty-six hours. We are calling up the army res—"

The screen turns black. I scramble for the remote and jab at the buttons. Nothing happens, so I try the light switch.

"They've cut our 'lectric'ty," Tig says.

＃

As the sun sets behind the tower, I force down some cold canned soup, thinking wistfully of the drawer full of take-away menus and my father's credit card. Tig only manages a couple of mouthfuls before pushing hers away, and I don't blame her. It's saltier and greasier for being cold.

I turn on my phone long enough to message Dad, tell him I won't be back today and not to worry. It's just as well. I can't face him right now. I ignore all the missed calls, and turn the phone back off. He's probably busy anyway. And pissed off at the Government for stealing his raid idea.

Then there's the grate of the bookcase being pushed back. I freeze, spoon halfway to my mouth. Galen steps into the room, head down, face hidden in shadows. He walks over to Tig and lays a hand on her forehead.

"Hmm. How are you feeling?"

"'Orrible. But I've been worse."

Galen places a kiss on her nose.

"What's it like out there?" I ask.

"Chaos. There are gangs stealing whatever they can. The tents have been ransacked, people are injured." He heads to some cupboards and picks dried leaves, bandages and pills from the shelves.

That explains the mess in the courtyard. I bite my lip.

"Will the girl be all right? Sophie? The one who was attacked?"

"I patched her up. She needs real help, but she can't leave. She's got to look after her dad. He got sentenced to polio years ago and now he's paralyzed. Plus, she's under a Level 2 Recall." He finishes packing the bag. "I have to go back out. Are you two okay?"

There's something up. Whatever it is, he's not going to tell me in front of Tig.

"Can I talk to you outside?" I point back at the bookcase.

He nods, and I follow him through to the other flat.

Galen faces the door, his back to me. "I'm sorry. I know I said I'd get you out of here as soon as possible, but things have changed."

"What's changed?"

"There are rumors that you're here. Someone saw you arrive. And it's more dangerous since they cut the power. People are getting desperate."

I look back at the bookcase. I can't leave Tig anyway.

"It's fine. Tig's a bit worse today. I'm happy to look after her."

Galen turns around. The skin around his left eye is dark purple, and a cut runs down from his forehead.

My hand goes to my mouth. "Who did that to you?"

"People who want medicine and painkillers. Don't worry, I cleaned it already. Make sure Tig gets lots of fluids, and encourage her to eat. I'll be back as soon as I can."

"Did you hear the news?" I ask.

He pauses with his hand on the doorknob.

"The Government is talking about a raid now. Not waiting until the election."

His shoulders slump. "I know. I've seen the army vans gathering outside. But we'll get you out before then."

"I'm not worried about me. What will happen to you?"

He shrugs. "That's a problem for another day. But I appreciate you taking care of Tig. It means a lot."

"You should stay. It's dangerous out there."

Galen shakes his head. "People will die without someone to treat them." He opens the door. "Lock this as soon as I'm gone. Get behind the bookcase, and keep quiet. Don't let anyone in, no matter what."

I lock the door behind him, wondering if I'll see him again.

CHAPTER TWENTY

BARBICAN,
LONDON
TWO DAYS LEFT

I PILE UP BLANKETS next to Tig's bed and sleep there, missing my memory foam mattress. I wake countless times, my hip and shoulders sore. I spend the next day trying to coax her into eating. She doesn't complain, just lies there, eyes glassy, nodding or shaking her head to my questions. I can't bear to turn my phone on. I hope Dad hasn't called the police.

The tiredness feels ground in, like dirt. Like the stains in the carpet, although it's clear Galen keeps it as clean as possible. It's sanitary, but the flat's old, and falling apart, and they obviously can't afford to replace anything. The wallpaper's peeling, the sofa's threadbare, and the plates are chipped.

I miss my clean flat. The warm bathroom floors, the deep bath. My double bed. The shining kitchen, and the cappuccino machine. There's only instant coffee here, but I make some with tepid water from the tap and manage to force it down. I need to stay awake, to watch over Tig and the flat.

I miss my dad too. But I try not to think about that.

The day lurches into evening without Galen's return.

What's happened to him?

It's almost completely dark when Tig wakes again. She's coughing hard, crying between breaths. I run to get water, but she shakes her head. She reaches for a tissue and coughs into it. Tig hands it to me, too weak to reach the bin. I make out dark stains on it. I take it to the window to catch the weak evening light.

Blood. She's coughing up blood.

Tears flow. What am I meant to do? She lapses back into sleep and I lay my hand on her head, like Galen did. She's unnaturally hot, like holding a mug of tea. Her pulse pounds through her skin. I try to count under my breath, but I can't keep up.

I head to the cupboards Galen got supplies from, and swing them open. Squinting through the gloom I spot bags of herbs and a couple of bottles of pills. No labels. I can't risk giving Tig pills without knowing what they are.

Pushing the bookcase back, I squeeze through and search the kitchen. Nothing.

I shut the cupboards. I'm as useless as I was when Rebecca died. I stand in the main flat for a long time, wondering what to do as the darkness closes in around me.

My hands clutch into fists. If Dad understood the reality of all this, surely he'd help. I can't believe the man who sat with me, night after night, when I was injured would abandon a child like Tig.

A scratching sound catches my attention. It's coming from my right, where the front door is. I creep toward the bookcase. I need to get back to Tig. There's a scraping noise followed by quiet swearing on the other side of the door. Then a faint click.

Someone is picking the lock.

My heart pounds, too loud in the darkness. I shuffle across the floor, the need to be silent slowing my steps. A few feet between me and the bookcase.

Do I have time to hide?

The clunk of the doorknob. Hinges creak.

"Shh," someone says.

"He's out," says a second whisperer.

"Could be hiding that politician chick. She asked for him on her way in."

I hold my breath. Muted footsteps. A circle of light bobs along the hallway wall, but it's still pitch black in the sitting room. I back toward the bookcase, reach behind me, and find the edge of it with my fingers. The light sweeps across the sitting room floor and I freeze.

Surely they saw me.

I'm not breathing. What will they do if they find me? I scan the room for a weapon. But there are only books within reach.

I have to move.

The light flashes around the walls, over the couch. One of the men drops down and shines it underneath.

Now is my chance. I move fast, squeezing behind the bookcase, flinching at the slight sound of my steps. The circle of light advances into the center of the room. Did they hear that?

"No one here. Check the other rooms."

I close my eyes for a moment. Thank goodness.

But I'm not safe. The bookcase is still away from the wall. The gap visible behind it.

How am I going to move it back into place?

Perhaps they won't notice. It's so dark in here, and their lights leave deep shadows. Maybe they won't come close.

"I'll start searching the kitchen. That's probably where he keeps the meds."

I swallow. If they're looking for Galen's drugs they'll turn this place upside down.

I have to move the bookcase.

I reach for the handle in the back and pull. There's a creak. I pause, breath held.

Footsteps from the corridor, coming back to the sitting room. A voice, no longer whispering. "All clear."

"Good. Let's get to it." Then comes the clatter of kitchen cabinets, the sound of crockery clinking.

Inch by inch I drag the bookcase back into place, glad that the scraping is covered by the noise the intruders are making. As soon as it's against the wall, I collapse against it.

More clatter from outside. The sound of smashing. I hurry to Tig's bed.

She's still breathing, thank God.

But it's shallow, slow. And she doesn't wake even as the clamor of the burglars grows louder, grows closer to the bookcase.

What am I going to do if they get in here? My fight with Galen's friends showed how pathetic I am. They probably ran off because they only meant to scare me in the first place.

There's a large, ceramic plant pot nearby. I scoop it up. I can swing it against a head, if they come in here. If I time it just right. But I don't know what I'll do about the second man.

The noise continues.

After a while I sit down, still clutching the pot in one arm. I stroke Tig's hair with the other, hoping she won't wake. She's damp with sweat. I pray they don't move the bookcase. Pray Tig doesn't cry out in her sleep. I want to cover my ears as the sound of smashing gets closer. A hollow, wooden sound makes me jump. They're on the other side of the bookcase, checking the shelves. I stare into the darkness, pot raised and ready.

But after a long time there's swearing, then the flat outside grows quiet again. I hold on to the pot for a long time before lowering it to the ground. I close my eyes and cry, feeling useless, trying to sob silently. After a long while, the tears dry up and the exhaustion of the last few days consumes me.

⨎

I awake with a jolt. The bookcase is scraping back. I fumble in the darkness for the pot.

"Tig! Talia!" Galen's voice is breathless.

"We're here!" I'm so glad it's him. I'm about to say we're okay. But we're not.

"What happened?" Galen bursts in, clutching a torch. He shines it in my face and I blink.

"People broke in. Looking for medicine."

"But they didn't find you? You're all right?"

"Tig's much worse. She was coughing up blood."

The torch's glare moves from my eyes and I'm blind for a second. Then Tig's pale face appears in the oval of light. Galen rushes to her side and puts a hand on her head.

"How long has she been like this?"

"Hours. Most of the day. Where have you been?"

"There was so much to do. I wanted to get back. I'm sorry. I didn't know she was this bad." He picks up her wrist and looks at his watch, counting.

"128." He swings his bag from his shoulder, and pulls out a y-shaped tube. He puts two ends into his ears and presses a metal circle against her chest, under her clothes. I watch his profile, intent on his sister. His Adam's apple bobs. I want to ask what's wrong with her, but he holds his finger to his lips as he listens, then swears.

"Get some water," he says, reaching in his bag.

When I get back with the cup, Galen sits Tig up. She's limp, but he shakes her. Her eyes open slowly and focus on me.

"Mum?" she says.

I reach out, pat her hand. "Sorry, sweetheart; it's me, Talia."

Her eyes are closing again.

"Swallow this, Tig." Galen lifts a pill to her lips, and I pass the cup. Once the pill has gone he lowers her. She's already asleep.

Galen points back at the bookcase, and we head through into

the main room. His light roams around the flat and I gasp at the devastation. The sofa cushions have been slashed. Broken crockery spills out of the kitchen. The sideboard has been smashed to pieces.

Galen shakes his head.

"I'm so glad you're okay," I say. "You were gone so long, I worried …"

He gives me a smile. "And I'm glad you're okay too."

We look at each other for a minute. I want to reach out for him. But now isn't the time.

"What's wrong with Tig?"

He pauses. "I think it's pneumonia."

I know that one's bad. You have to go to Quarantine. People die of it.

"Will that pill help?"

"That's just a painkiller. It'll bring her temperature down. It's not enough. We need antibiotics. But my suppliers are all out." He runs his fingers through his hair. "I can give her water, try to keep her fever down for now. But she needs real help."

His eyes are glistening, only half his face visible in the torchlight.

"Is there anything I can do?"

He shakes his head. "We need to get you out of the Barbican. It's getting worse."

"I don't want to leave Tig."

"You don't have to." He kicks at a piece of mug. "The deadline for the raid is tomorrow afternoon. There are army vans gathering all around the estate. As soon as they break through, you should take Tig to them. They'll take care of you both."

I'm about to say they'll put her in a home. But it's clear from his face he knows it.

"Her only chance is antibiotics," he says.

"Or the Transfer."

A bitter laugh. "And possibly kill another person? She wouldn't want that. Anyway, with us criminals all locked up here, the waitlist is too long."

His head is hanging. Once the army gets hold of him, they'll put him in Quarantine. He may never see her again. But he's right. It's her only chance.

BARBICAN,
LONDON
ONE DAY LEFT

GALEN AND I FALL asleep propped up against
Tig's bed. He's snoring in minutes, his warmness comforting as he
slumps against me. I listen to them both breathe, hoping Tig will
make it. Hoping tomorrow won't be too late.

I wake as the sun comes through the windows. The greenery
tangles my senses, and for a moment I think I'm in a forest. Galen's
head is resting against my neck, his breath soft on my skin. I can see
his mouth, his stubble, his expression so open, so at peace.

I ease his limp form to the ground. He murmurs, but doesn't
wake as I lie him down and turn to Tig. I put a hand to her forehead and her eyelids flutter, but don't open. She's just as hot. The pill
didn't work, or wore off.

She needs those antibiotics now.

But there are still hours to go and I can't sit still, can't wait for
the two of them to wake. I move the bookcase softly and creep
into the other flat. I find some bin bags under the sink and start
picking up the mess in the sitting room. It's probably a waste of time.
Who knows what the army will do to this flat? I put anything I think
could be mended on the table.

This place is so different to my home. The penthouse doesn't even feel real anymore. It's become a vision of heaven. Clean, warm, luxurious. Has Dad been back there? Does he worry about where I am, or is he relieved to have me out of the way?

I've made a lot of headway when Galen appears through the gap in the bookcase.

"Wow," he says. "Did you do all this while I was asleep?"

"Just wanted to be useful. I noticed how clean the flat was before." I reach for a shard of broken plate.

"Thanks. Mum was a maid, so she was particular about cleaning. It wore off on me."

I drop the fragment into the bag and straighten. "What happened to her? If you don't mind me asking."

"Knocked down by a car on the way home five years ago." His voice has a catch in it. "Guy who hit her had good lawyers, said it was a mistake — he wasn't a real criminal and he deserved a second chance. He only got a stomach bug. The rich always get off lightly."

I don't know what to say as Galen continues. I had a good lawyer too.

"It's one law for them, one for us. They need an underclass to be permanently sick. So we don't make 'mistakes' like they do. They call us evil, criminals. No second chances."

"Everyone deserves a second chance."

"And the rich get them. But young black men from the Barbican don't. We don't even get first chances. Most people assume we must be sick as soon as they see us and cross the road."

He's got a point. Employers won't touch Barbican residents. Even if they have no record. They assume they're guilty of something, they just haven't been caught yet.

And I made that assumption when I saw Galen's trainers.

"I never thought about that."

"You never had to. They want people with nice addresses — and phone numbers, so they can call them in at short notice."

"Phone numbers?"

"The phone companies won't install landlines here. And we can't afford mobiles. Do you know how much those cost?"

I actually don't. Dad pays my bill.

Galen continues. "Most people don't understand stuff like that. They haven't been here. Sebastian Conway has."

"He's been here?"

"Met the people. Listened to the stories. He wants to help. And when he took over the Democratic Justice Party, it gave us all hope. But then your father's party started gaining in the polls."

I bite my lip. "I … I don't support him anymore. Dad, I mean." I feel guilty saying it, like I'm betraying him. "I know that doesn't count for much, but it's the truth. I still love him, but I want Sebastian Conway to win."

"He's your father," Galen says. "It counts for a lot. And it means something to me."

"He's not a bad man. It started with him wanting to prevent what happened to Mum and Rebecca happening to anyone else. But somewhere along the line it became about revenge."

We look at each other for a long time. His green eyes are intent on mine. Then he takes a deep breath. "I'd better get Tig another painkiller."

We head back through the gap. Galen tries to wake Tig, but she's beyond drowsy. She can't open her eyes for more than a few seconds. It takes a long time to get her to swallow her pill. Once she's lying back on the bed, Galen paces the leafy room like a tiger.

"The antibiotics will help, won't they?" I ask.

"Maybe. But the sooner she gets them the better," Galen says, stopping by Tig's bed. "I'll borrow a stretcher, and together with a couple of my mates we can get her downstairs, but then we'll have to hide and you'll be on your own."

"What mates?"

"I'll message Gazzer."

"Gazzer? Where have I heard that name?"

Galen avoids my eyes and strokes his sister's forehead. "You punched him."

"No. Not him."

"He's one of my best friends," Galen says. "I'd trust him with my life."

"And that guy with the neck tattoo? I saw him on TV shouting at the police. He's crazy."

"Yeah, Reece is a bit nuts at times. Tyler will help too."

I swallow. "I can't imagine they're fans of mine."

"Nah. Definitely not." He meets my gaze. "But Gazzer'll take care of you and Tig. Trust me."

"I trust you. It's him I'm worried about."

⨎

The raid deadline is this afternoon, so the boys are coming over before it kicks off, while it's still safe for them to travel across the estate. We spend the morning waiting. People come to the door and I hide behind the bookcase, listening to Galen explain he has to stay with Tig, listen to him give advice, bandages, and painkillers.

When it's quiet, we sit together by his sister's bed. Sometimes talking, sometimes silent. I keep catching his eye, accidentally. I want to reach out for him, to feel his breath on my neck again, but I don't know what to say.

After a while Galen heads into the other room. He comes back with a bag and hands it to me.

"You'd better get ready," he says. I peer into it. There are my clothes. The red jumper and tweed skirt I arrived in, cleaned. I head into the bedroom in the main flat, get changed and tidy my hair.

There's a knock on the bedroom door.

"Come in," I say, and Galen enters.

He looks me up and down. "Yup, that's the Talia Hale the army will recognize."

"Are your friends here yet?"

"Nah. But at least I get a chance to thank you." He walks over, takes both my hands. "I appreciate this." His gaze is hard on me, his hands warm around mine. "It's Tig's best chance."

"It's nothing." I can't look away. "After all I've put you through, it's the least I can do."

"You've been trying to help."

"And where did it get you? All this is my fault. Are you sure you still trust me to help?"

Galen leans forward. I'm breathless as his face grows close. But he whispers in my ear.

"I trust you," he says. Then he pulls back, slowly, the soft stubble of his cheek against my skin, until his lips are an inch away. I can't stand it anymore, and I lean in and kiss him.

His lips are softer than I'd imagined. He drops my hands, and pulls me close, an arm tight around my waist. For a moment, there's only him. The brush of his skin, the scent of him.

That's when the doorbell rings.

"Damn," he says, his mouth still close against mine.

Galen gives me a smile as I pull away, then goes to answer the door. I stand for a moment, feeling the tingling though my body.

Deep voices from the hall. Laughter. I hurry to join Galen, feeling awake — fully awake — for the first time in longer than I can remember.

It's the guys. Galen exchanges complicated handshakes with them as they enter the flat. I wonder if I'm blushing.

"Talia," Galen says. "Gazzer, Reece, and Tyler."

The guys stare at me.

"She'll get Tig to the army. It's well simple. Help her get Tig down the stairs, but stay out of sight. Talia'll get help from the squaddies."

Galen speaks with more of an East London accent with them.

The guys still stare at me. I stare back, still stuck in the moment, in the kiss, the feeling of being alive.

It's almost a relief when the noises start. Helicopters, shouts, and screams. Smashing glass. Bang on time. The boys flinch, and without a word we head to the balcony and lean over. I see Galen clutch the edge so tight his knuckles turn white. I'm not surprised.

It's an invasion.

The main barricade must be down, because there are camouflage uniforms streaming into the Barbican from the direction of London Wall. There's a group of residents standing shoulder to shoulder in the courtyard and, as the soldiers approach them, they toss flaming bottles that explode when they hit the ground. Petrol bombs. But the army keeps coming behind, holding their riot shields in front of them, almost dancing on the spot to put the flames out, helped by a couple of soldiers following with fire extinguishers. Smoke bursts out in patches by the residents, then they're running away, hands over their eyes. Tear gas. They're helping each other. Arms pulled over shoulders. An injured man carried between three people.

The tear gas keeps coming until the courtyard is hazy with it.

The residents have fled. They never had a chance. The ones that couldn't run fast enough are being dragged toward London Wall by the soldiers, or beaten as they lie on the ground. A short while ago I'd have been impressed at the efficiency of our boys in uniform. Now I stand slack-jawed and helpless as they march into the center of the Barbican.

They're going for one of the lower buildings. The door is already smashed so they run right in, more than I can count.

There's a chill running through me. We can't take Tig into that gas. Who knows what it'll do to her weakened lungs? And how would I ask them for help? They're not going to recognize me through the riot gear and gas. They'll think I'm a threat.

Galen is rubbing his forehead. He stops and points.

"Mrs. Onyango!"

I follow his finger back to the low building. Some of the soldiers are coming out, bringing people with them. Galen is pointing at an elderly lady, barely able to keep up with the two soldiers who half-march, half-drag her out.

Gazzer's fists are balled at his sides. He's hoping from one foot to another like he wants to jump off the balcony and go fight the soldiers.

Galen swears. "She's never broken a law in her life. She's got Alzheimer's, and I've been trying to help with her osteoporosis." He faces me. "They're going to break her bones! She's so fragile."

There's a knot in my stomach, and I turn back to the scene, wishing I could do something. But what can I do? The courtyard is a pen of violence and desperation.

"We can't take Tig down there," I say.

Galen drops his head in his hands. Turns away from us.

"Well, I'm gonna get down there," Gazzer says. "I'm giving those scum the fight of their lives."

"No. You'll lose. We'll all lose," Galen says, muffled by his hands. He sniffs. "You should get out of here. You too, Talia."

"There's no way out. Anyway, I'm not leaving you and Tig. We'll be safe in the hidden flat. They're not going to find it in full riot gear."

"I'm not running," Reece says. "This is our home."

"There is a way out," Galen says. "Some people have been sneaking out over one of the barriers by St. Barts. People under Level 1 Recalls mostly, frightened of the consequences if they don't report to hospital. It's risky, but it's your best bet. It's not well guarded."

"Then we'll take Tig out that way."

He shakes his head. "There's climbing involved. And running. There's no way you'd make it with Tig. And there's nothing any of you can do here to help."

I turn away from him and clutch the balcony, watching the

soldiers drag people from their homes. He's right. There's nothing I can do here. Nothing any of us can do for Tig without antibiotics.

Antibiotics.

"St. Barts!"

The guys all look at me.

I grab Galen's arm. "They're giving out antibiotics there, remember? We don't need to take Tig to the antibiotics. We can bring the antibiotics to Tig!"

His green eyes meet mine. They widen.

"I can get some. Try to get them back here, back to you. Do you think I'll be able to get back in the way I'm getting out?"

Galen shakes his head. "Not a chance. Getting out is risky enough."

Dammit. We're so close. I breathe in through my nose, hard. But when I look at Galen again, he's smiling.

"It's not you that needs to get back in, though. It's the pills."

"What?"

"There's a wall at Beech Street. Away from the barricades and the buildings, so it should be clear. If you can get the antibiotics, I can be there at, say, six to catch them if you throw them up."

"No," that's Reece. "What'll happen to Tig if they catch you and you don't come back?"

Galen squeezes his eyes closed, swears. "It's worth the risk."

"Nah. Not for you. But for us it is. I'll be there to get the pills," Gazzer says. "I didn't want to leave, either way."

"Me too," Tyler adds. "If those squaddies try to stop us, we'll beat them down."

Galen looks like he wants to throw his arms around his mates. But he sticks his hands in his pockets instead.

"Can't ask you to do that."

"You're not asking. We're doing," Tyler says.

I bite my lip. There are so many things that can go wrong. But what other choice do we have?

"How do I get out?"

"Guys, can you get her to the barricade? You'll have to climb, then run like hell. There are riot police on the other side."

Reece looks me up and down. "I can get the meds from St. Barts. Throw them up to the lads. You can't trust her kind."

I open my mouth, but Galen speaks before I can.

"I trust her," he says. "And if they ask for ID at the hospital, what are you gonna do, Reece? Surrender for your Recall? Run and risk being shot?"

The guys stare at each other, and I wonder what Reece did.

"Fine," Reece says after a long pause.

"I'm going to say goodbye to Tig, then."

I duck into the flat and climb through to the hidden room. The afternoon light dapples on her still face. The room is quiet. For a moment my heart stops, but then I see her chest, rising and falling, silently.

I cross to the bed. "Don't worry," I say, stroking her hair. "I won't let you down." I place a kiss on her hot forehead before heading back out to join the others.

"What are we waiting for?" Gazzer says. "The army will be here soon."

I peer down. He's wrong. They're cleaning out the lower buildings first. We still have time. Hopefully enough to get the meds to Galen.

"Yeah. I guess you should get going." Galen drops his eyes.

I swallow. I want to kiss him again, be near him, say goodbye properly. But there's no way that's happening now. The wind blows smoke in my face, stinging my eyes.

"I won't let you down," I say.

"I know."

"Move it," Reece says. "Tick tock."

Galen follows us back into the flat and opens the front door. The boys go through first. Galen gives me a tight smile as I leave.

It's so hard to turn away from him. When will I see him again?

The guys are noisy going down the stairs. Reece whoops and slides down the banisters. I hurry to keep up. By the time we reach the foyer, I'm coughing. Gazzer stops suddenly in front of the broken doors. I almost run into him.

"I can't stand posh birds like you," he says. "Think you're our great white savior." He shakes his head. "But you make it worse, because you don't understand us, don't want to listen to us."

I don't know what to say to that. I did make things worse.

"You'll let us down. Girls like you always bail when things get tough. Don't wanna break your nails."

"I'll get the antibiotics," I say, but my voice is weak.

He laughs. "Yeah, right. Run home to Daddy, you will."

There's no time to argue with him. Outside, there's the clamor from across the Barbican. Shouts, screams, and the clatter of thrown bottles.

"Just be there at six," I say.

Tyler opens the doors. The sky is the gray of tombstones. Helicopters hover over London Wall.

"Get out there," Gazzer says, and he gives me a push.

I STUMBLE OUT INTO the courtyard. For a moment, I think the guys have abandoned me, but they appear on either side, walking fast. The action is across the square, but we're in the shadows. Cocooned by the darkness and the smoke from the petrol bombs and tear gas. My eyes itch as though I'm been rubbing at them.

"This way, princess," Gazzer says.

"Hold on." I pull out my phone and swipe to the camera. I zoom in on the action across from us. It's hazy, but clear enough to be horrifying. They're dragging a woman across the courtyard by one arm. She's clutching a tiny baby with her free hand and straining toward a toddler thrown over the shoulder of another soldier. The toddler's face is red, hair stuck to its wet face as it screams. Once I get the antibiotics, I can show this footage to someone. Try to get help. They're clearly not checking to see who is under a Recall and who isn't.

Reece tries to grab my phone. "What the hell?"

"Bloody tourist," Tyler says.

"One minute." I straighten up the shot and capture a bit more of the scene. An elderly couple, the man being marched too fast to be able to use his stick properly. He crumples to the ground. A couple of school-age children keeping up with the soldiers, eyes wide, parents nowhere in sight.

Gazzer grabs my phone. "You've had your fun."

I snatch it back. "People need to know what's happening here."

Reece snorts. "They don't care. Now move it. That way. As soon as we're out of the shadows, run."

I shove my phone back in my pocket and focus on the concrete to avoid tripping. There's mess everywhere. I step in a red-brown stain but keep going.

We reach the edge of the tower's shadow. There's nowhere else to hide.

"This way!" Tyler pulls at my arm, and we're running.

Rubbish blows past me, fragments of the barricade and the remainder of the cardboard city that used to be here. Paper and plastic whipped up in the vortex created by the towers. A sheet of newspaper sticks to my leg, a picture of my father plastered across the front. I almost trip to avoid stepping on his face.

I'm falling behind. I didn't pick these shoes for running. They're too loose, and they flap at my heels as I try to keep pace with the thudding of the guys' footsteps.

"Come on!" Gazzer shouts. I resist the urge to shout back. I need my breath. It's coming hard now, given a sharp edge from the gas. Like shards in my lungs.

There's the barrier. A heap of junk like a weird nest, jammed between two tall buildings. Tyler cranes back over his shoulder, looking past me. He swears, and runs faster. I don't need to look back, I can hear the footsteps now myself. The thud of heavy boots, still some distance away. They've seen us. They're coming.

But we're at the barrier. It's clear why this is the escape route. Narrow stairs lead down to the street, but the riot cops on the other side can't get too close. We're overlooked by the buildings, and there are open windows. I can see a woman leaning out of one of them, blond hair in her face, tapping a bottle on the windowsill. The cops huddle behind their riot shields, the ground glittering with broken glass and scorch marks.

"Get her over," Tyler says. "Then get out of here."

We're at the barricade. Tyler is next to me, bent over, fingers laced together by my feet.

"Come on!"

I slip my foot into his hands, and he boosts me up. I clutch at the barricade, searching for a handhold.

There's a bang and something metallic clatters on the ground. I shove my hand into a gap, and pull myself up.

"Tear gas!" Reece shouts. I peer down. Smoke streams from the grenade. The boys back away, pull out handkerchiefs. I drag myself to the top of barricade. My eyes sting. I reach for another grip, but the barricade is blurring. Shouts, as our pursuers catch up.

Swearing, Tyler's. Then grunts and the muffled thump of kicks and punches.

My foot slips. A hand clutches at my ankle from the Barbican side.

I kick out, but the gas is suffocating me. It's hard to hold on, hard to focus on anything other than the burning in my eyes and throat and lungs. I squeeze my eyes shut.

Another shout, a thump, and someone cries out. The hand releases me. I pull myself back up and swing my feet over to the other side of the barricade. I try for a foothold on the way down, but can't find any. My grip slips.

I fall down the other side of the barricade, into the city.

I've barely landed when there's a blow, a sudden pain flaring through my right side.

I roll over, open my eyes. A shadowy shape looms above me, gas mask on, riot shield in front and truncheon raised. The police. I push up on my hands and knees and scramble to the side. The next blow hits the concrete next to me.

Then there's a crash and a clatter. I catch a flash of the scene before the pain forces my eyes closed again. Another smashed bottle on the ground. A triumphant shout comes from the window above me.

I start crawling away, coughing, spluttering, hoping I'm hidden in the tear gas. The stab of glass in my hand. Then I'm on my feet again. I open my eyes for one second, to check my path is clear, then run, blind. The shouting grows faint behind me. I hit something and land hard on the ground, choking. I pry open my eyes and stare at the blue of a wheelie bin. I drag myself behind it.

I wipe a sleeve across my face. It's doesn't do much good. I'm drooling, crying, and my nose is running. I pull myself up against the wall, blindly, and start retching.

I rest my hand on my thigh, concentrate on breathing until I can open my eyes a little. They sting like hell and my nose is still running, but I can hold them open for a second or two at a time. That will be enough. I glance at my injured hand, at the shard of glass wedged in my palm, near the scar Galen sewed up. It's not too big. Won't need stitches this time. I grit my teeth and pull it out. Try not to cry, not that it matters, since my face is already streaming with tears.

This wasn't the plan, but I'm out of the Barbican, at least. I hope Galen's friends got away. I hope they're okay. I hope they'll be there at six.

There's no way to check. I have to get to St. Barts.

CHAPTER TWENTY-THREE

St. Barts,
London
One Day Left

I CUT DOWN THE hazy streets, blinking constantly, the world strobing around me. Thank goodness St. Barts isn't far. I run past the back entrance, and almost get hit by a blur of a van. I stumble back onto the curb as another roars past, the back covered in the blobby brown-green of camouflage fabric.

Army vans.

I stop and get out my phone. They pull up at the back door to St. Barts, where Mike picked me up after my transfer. Soldiers are waiting, and people are dragged out of the back of the van. I try to focus, but I can't make out their faces. They're fuzzy shapes. But there's a woman desperately trying to keep a towel around herself, obviously dragged out mid-shower. A teenage boy is thrown to the ground, and sprawls on his side. An old black man pulls himself up straight and waves away the soldier as he tries to get down by himself, but the soldier grabs his wrist, and almost yanks him over as he hands him to the soldiers at the hospital.

They're taking people straight from the Barbican to receive transfers.

They can't do this.

What happened to due process? They clearly haven't bothered to weed out the innocent from the guilty.

"Hey!" one of the soldiers shouts. I can't tell if it's at me or not, but I shove my phone in my pocket and walk away quickly, heading for the main entrance. I can't get caught now, but I think I got enough. Once I've handed over the antibiotics, I'm going to show this to people. Make them see what's going on.

I stumble through the tunnel under Henry VIII, and into the foyer. In the hospital, I remember where the ladies' loos are and rush for them. Inside, I splash my face with water. It helps. I can make out my reflection in the mirror. Red-rimmed eyes, only half open, nose still running. But looking a mess isn't a bad thing. I'm meant to be ill, after all. I rinse the glass cut on my hand, grab a paper towel, and press it to my palm until the bleeding stops completely.

I straighten my skirt and tidy my hair. Was it less than a month ago I was here as a law-abiding patient? I push the bathroom door open and step into the modern grandeur of the space. My side aches from the truncheon blow.

I hold my head high, playing the part of the girl I used to be. I try not to blink too often. But my eyes sting, and everything is blurred.

The air buzzes with disgruntled voices. A lineup snakes away from the reception desk, the people lumpy blobs from here.

In the center of the foyer the blurry figures of two nurses stand by a table handing out white packages from a stack of large boxes.

Antibiotics.

I join the queue at the table. Everyone faces straight ahead, leaving a few feet of distance between themselves and the people ahead of them.

The line moves slowly. I shift from foot to foot. I don't have time for this. I need to be back for my six o'clock meeting to throw the pills over the wall to the boys. But my eyes open more as I wait, and my nose dries up a little. The nurses at the front talk to each patient in turn, and each walks away with a package.

This should be easy.

When I finally reach the front, the nurse holds her hand out. "Diagnosis, please," she says.

"What?"

She tilts her head in sympathy. "You do look under the weather, love. If you'll give me your diagnosis, I'll get you sorted out."

"I ... I don't have a diagnosis."

"Didn't you see the sign? You have to check in at reception, have a blood test, and bring us the results. No point in giving you broad-spectrum antibiotics if it's a virus. You'll have to join the wait for a Transfer in that case."

"I didn't see the sign. But they're not for me. I came to pick them up for a friend."

"Your friend has to come here and have a blood test like anyone else."

I shake my head. "She can't, she's too ill to come in."

Her eyes narrow. "Then you should have called an ambulance."

I want to punch something. The queue at reception is worse. And once I reach the front, my blood test will be negative. They'll never give me the medicine.

I pull myself up straight, and put on my best "daughter of the future prime minister" face.

"Do you know who I am?" I say, hating the words even as they come out.

The nurse meets my look with a steely-eyed gaze of her own. "Yes. A spoiled politician's daughter who thinks the rules don't apply to her."

My shoulders slump.

But the antibiotics lie in the box, two feet away. A white bag, ready to go. That's all I need.

I lean forward. Snatch at the package. Then I'm running. Shoes flapping on my feet. The paper bag crinkling in my hand.

I get about six paces before the shouting starts.

"Hey! Stop!" It's the nurse. I keep running.

Footsteps behind me. Heavy ones. A male voice.

"Freeze! Drop the pills!"

My breath obeys him, stopping in my throat, but my legs keep running. The automatic doors open. A family walks though.

"Police! Stop or I'll shoot!"

Oh no.

I'm in a hospital. There's a shoot-to-kill policy. But I'm at the door. A crack, and screaming. A dull impact on my right arm. Like a punch. The antibiotics slip out of my hand and skid across the floor, under a café table.

"No!" Someone shouts. Maybe the nurse.

Have I been shot?

I'm about to lunge for the pills. But I can see the officer in the corner of my eye. He's still pointing his gun at me. Lining it up.

I can't go back for them.

The family entering the hospital stands in my way, statues frozen in the open doors.

"Hold your fire!" A different voice: male. "You'll hit them!"

I shove through the still life of the family. My arm feels numb. I dash into the courtyard, put my hand on my sleeve. It's wet. Security guards run toward me and, for a second, I think I'm caught. But they run right past and into the foyer.

My red jumper hides the blood; it just looks damp. They don't know who they're chasing. They're responding to the shots.

I slow down. Try to look casual. As the second group of guards runs by I shout, "He's in there!" and point toward the hospital.

I get to the archway, jog through the tunnel under the building, and emerge onto the main road from beneath Henry VIII. I mingle with the crowds, lowering my head.

My blood is pumping, soaking through my jumper. The pain kicks in, taking my breath. I press down on the wound to slow the flow, but it hurts too much. I stumble along Newgate toward St. Paul's, trying to blend in.

What now? The pain is building in waves. I focus on the pavement as I walk, breathing through my teeth. I can't go to an ER department. They'll arrest me, I'll end up in Quarantine.

I still need antibiotics for Tig. But there's no other hospital for miles. And what would I do if I made it? Steal more pills? It's probably past six o'clock. The boys at the Barbican will have given up on me. Will think I've run away. And there's no way I can get past the police and climb the barricades with my arm like this.

Tig might die.

No. I won't let that happen.

Blood drips from my arm as I walk. I don't know how much longer I can keep going.

The crowds are thicker by St. Paul's. I lean against a wall. It's all hopeless. I watch the people passing by, but they blur into gray. I feel dizzy. I don't know if it's the pain or the bleeding or the tear gas.

A man with a mustache forces the free afternoon paper onto people as they head into the station. He tries to give one to me, but I hold my upper arm tightly. So he slips it into the crook of my elbow with a wink.

"Are you okay, love?" he asks.

I don't trust myself to speak, so I push off from the wall and keep going. I have to sit down. The churchyard. I get through the gate and stagger to a spot behind a tree. It's not hidden, but I'll be less noticeable there. I collapse onto the ground, dropping the paper, the jolt of my body sending a wave of pain through my arm. I bite my tongue to hold down the scream and hunch over to hide my face, still clutching my injured arm.

Then I let myself cry.

Why is this happening to me again? Isn't being shot once enough? I start sobbing, facing the tree, hoping no one will notice. Hoping they'll leave me here.

Tig will probably die. Galen will end up in Quarantine. And it's all my fault.

I may die too. Bleed out in St. Paul's churchyard. There are worse places. And I'm useless now, unable to save Tig. Will they even know I tried? Or will the boys think they were right, that I headed home?

No, it'll be on the news at least. "Talia Hale Found Dead in Park." Galen will know I tried. Dad will be sad. He'll wish he'd listened to me. Knowing I sat here and bled to death.

It suddenly occurs to me how dumb that is. Of course Dad would be sad. Maybe even heartbroken. But he'd also think I'm an idiot for not getting help. And he'd be right. I don't need to die here. This is pathetic. This is self-pity. This isn't helping anyone.

I have to do better than this. If I die, I'm going to die trying. But what can I do? I straighten up, wipe my face on my sleeve. Look around.

The paper is lying next to me. Dad's face peers out from above the fold. I stare at the familiar features, feeling far from home. If Dad were here he'd help me.

Wait.

Dad can help me. Dad can get antibiotics. He has connections. He won't let Tig die, surely? And once I've got help for her, I'll happily go to a hospital. Cheerfully go to Quarantine and take whatever disease they want to give me.

And maybe, at the end of it all, Dad will let me come home.

Maybe.

The election is tomorrow. So he'll be on *Sharpe* this evening. That was the deal, for my softball interview. I glance at the time on my phone, ignoring the messages. A call won't be enough, and my battery might die completely. I have to see him in person.

Five past six. Less than an hour till my father is on air.

CHAPTER TWENTY-FOUR

THE WALK IS TORTURE. Pain radiates from my arm, a blunt agony, compounded as each footstep reverberates up my body. The arm of my jumper is soaking wet now, and the dampness has spread across half my chest. Red seeps through my fingers where I'm gripping my arm, and a few people glance at me strangely.

So at first I'm glad when it starts to rain as I turn onto the Embankment. It'll clean my hand, and wash away the trail of blood behind me. But as it starts to come down harder it's like it's washing away the last of my strength. My teeth chatter.

I want to rest. Want to give up, lie down. But I can't.

The stain fades from my jumper as the rain makes the wet universal. The chill of the water is slowing the blood flow, too. The liquid that drips from my jumper is pink, but it doesn't show on my tweed brown skirt.

It's getting harder to walk, veering too close to the curb, then too close to buildings. My feet are heavy and my thoughts clouded. I keep my head down as I merge with the tourists gawping at the Houses of Parliament.

I want to plan what I'm going to do when I see Dad, how I'm going to convince him. But my thoughts are as hard to hold on to as smoke. I'm drowsy.

He has to help.

I've zoned out so much it's a surprise when I see the television studios. I pull myself up straight, and focus as best I can. I head in through the front doors, grit my teeth and wave to the receptionist.

"Talia Hale," I say, making my voice as strong as I can. "I'm here to meet my father."

Yup. That's my whole plan. The receptionist takes in my drowned rat appearance. She clearly recognizes me. She checks a piece of paper and her brow furrows.

"You're not on the list."

"There must be a mistake."

She picks up the phone and leans back, talking quietly. She waits a long time for the response. I can't imagine what the reaction is in the Green Room, but they won't leave me in the foyer.

I'm dripping blood on the carpet. I'm lucky it's dark maroon.

After a while, she hangs up, and redials.

She covers the receiver and leans forward, speaking loudly enough for me to hear. "He's about to go on air, but they've asked me to send you up. I'll get you an escort."

I nod, biting my lip. I can't be impatient now.

My escort only takes a minute, a young guy in a badly fitting suit. Probably an intern.

"This way, please," he says. I follow him, almost losing my balance on my first step. He leads me to the lift. The pain feels slightly removed now, as if it's happening to someone else. I can focus a little better, but only on one thing at a time. Like watching my escort press the button for the right floor. Watching the numbers count up in the little display above the door. Stepping out carefully, and heading down the long corridor.

I let the young guy walk slightly ahead of me. He doesn't see me bump into the wall, or the red stain I leave on it. I still have my hand clamped to my arm, but the warm blood is seeping out slowly now, not flowing like before. I take my hand off and wipe it on my jumper. I don't want people questioning me, not when I'm so close.

He gets to the door of the Green Room and knocks on it. Piers opens it immediately, leaning on his cane. He must have been waiting right behind it.

"We can take over from here," he says. "Thank you."

My escort nods and leaves.

"Where the hell have you been?" Piers says as soon as the young man is out of earshot. "Get in here." He pulls me in by my good arm and kicks the door shut.

And there, standing in the center of the room, is my dad.

I want to run to him. To hide in his arms, and have him look after me, like he did after I was shot last time. But too much has changed. And he can't know I'm wounded now. So I just stand there.

And he runs to me.

I've never seen him move that fast. I only have time to turn to the side so he doesn't hug my injured arm.

"Oh Talia. Talia. Talia," he breathes into my hair. And he holds me like that. After a while, I realize he's shaking.

"Dad?" I manage. He pulls away. His eyes are wet.

"Are you okay?"

"Fine," I lie. "Just tired."

"Thank God." He closes his eyes for a moment.

"What the hell were you thinking?" Piers steps forward. "Malcolm was determined to call the police. Fortunately I convinced him you were just acting up. Can you imagine the scandal?"

Dad grabs a chair and pulls it over to me.

"Sit down. Where have you been?" he says.

I sink onto the white cushion gratefully, cringing as the movement sends a spasm of agony through my arm.

"Barbican," I manage. "The girl, Tig. She needs antibiotics. She might die. You've got to get the Government to stop the raid."

Piers's eyes are wide. "You've been in the Barbican? With all that's been going on?" He starts to pace. "This is bad, Talia. We can't let this get out."

"Please. You must be able to do something. Get medicine for her, get the army to let someone bring it in."

"No special treatment," Piers says. "Especially not for criminals. What kind of a message would that send?"

"Who cares?" I grit my teeth. "We can't let her die!"

Dad shakes his head. He looks sad. "I'm sorry. But we're not the Government yet. We have no control over the raid."

"But you're winning! You can offer them a coalition. Or committee appointments, isn't that what it's all about? New Year's Honors?"

"You know I can't do that on my own. And the party would never support it."

Piers butts in. "We need to manage this. Did anyone see you enter or leave?"

I'm cold. And we're getting off topic.

"They're rounding people up and taking them straight to have the Transfer." I pull out my phone. Swipe to bring up the footage from the Barbican, hit play, and hand it to Dad. "They're innocent people. And that's illegal."

Piers snorts. "Not since the Government stole our bloody idea."

Dad's still watching the video.

"What idea?"

"Martial law. Emergency measures," Piers says.

Dad hands me back the phone. "This isn't great, Talia, but some force is necessary sometimes …." He sounds uneasy, but I barely hear him. Blood is rushing in my ears. There's mist at the edge of my vision.

Piers keeps talking. "Everyone in the Barbican could have left when the barricades went up. By staying there, they're helping criminals avoid the Recall, avoid justice for their victims."

Dad runs his fingers through his hair.

"You're not going to help?"

He glances at the floor. "Maybe we can look at some exceptions once we've won the election. It does seem like there may be some special cases ..."

"That will be too late! Tig is sick now!"

"We're not in power now."

I slump back in the seat. "Tig is Rebecca's age. You won't let her die, will you, Dad?"

"I ... I'm not sure what I can do."

"You must be able to think of something!" But he doesn't respond. My head is fuzzy. "Dad ..."

The door opens and Alison walks in, along with a man with a clipboard. Her mouth falls open when she sees me. She stares for a moment, then a huge grin sweeps across her face.

"Talia! I'm so glad ...." She pauses, glances at the stranger to her left. "I'm so glad you were able to make it here for the show."

"It's time, Mr. Hale," the man says.

Dad turns to me. "We'll talk about this after."

"No ... Dad ...." But he's already heading out of the door, following Alison and the man with the clipboard.

The adrenaline is leaving me. I'm tired. Sleepy, even. The room is spinning a little. Am I going to pass out now? The pulse of pain in my arm is strong.

I have to do something. He'll be on the show for an hour. I'm not going to stay conscious that long. I'll be whisked off to hospital, to Quarantine. But what can I do?

I don't know, but I'm not giving up.

I push myself to my feet, clutching my arm.

"What are you doing?" Piers asks. Then he stops, and puts a hand to his mouth. I follow his gaze to the chair. The white cushion is now vivid red.

"You're injured. Dammit, Talia, what have you got yourself into? We'll need to get you treated. Discreetly."

I stumble toward the door to the studio. I'm not thinking straight. But this is the only plan I have. And I want to be near Dad, more than anything.

"Where are you going?"

I ignore him and keep walking. The thump of his cane comes from behind me.

"I can't let you go out there. Not in this state."

Piers reaches for my shoulder but I shrug him off, almost knocking him over.

"No! You'll ruin everything!"

My hand is on the handle.

"Talia!" He grabs me hard, on my wound. I cry out, but wrench out of his grasp and pull at the door.

"Stop! No one can see you like this!"

His hand is back on my injured arm. He's spotted the weakness. He squeezes, hard.

Pain knifes through my body. Hot liquid flows down my arm. Whatever clot formed is gone. I drop to my knees. Blackness creeps into the edge of my vision.

"Please ...." I can't fight. The agony crowds out my thoughts. A click comes from somewhere, then a creak of hinges.

"Sorry, Talia. I can't let you do this." Piers squeezes harder. I scream, but the sound feels distant. Like it's coming from the end of a long corridor. I'm falling sideways.

"What are you doing?" That's not Piers's voice. It's too high. "Leave her alone!"

My head is on the floor.

"Is that blood?"

I'm so cold. He doesn't let go.

"She's hurt! What the hell is wrong with you? Let her go!"

Everything is going dark.

There's a thud. A cry, and the release of the agony. Heat flows back into the wound and I lie there, the pain pulsing with my blood. My vision is coming back. The shape of the door resolves itself in front of me. It's open.

"Talia!"

Alison is at my side. Where did she come from? I push myself up. My bad arm screams in pain. The room lurches around me. Piers is on the floor, eyes squeezed shut. Mouth open in a silent scream. His walking stick lies a couple of yards away. I struggle to make sense of the scene.

"You kicked away Piers's cane?"

"I heard you shouting. What the hell happened? What was he doing to you?"

I have to think fast.

"He went crazy and attacked me!" I say. He's moaning on the floor, reaching for his leg. Oblivious to us in his agony.

Alison points at the blood pooling on the floor beside me. "He did this? I'll call an ambulance."

I get to my feet. The room spins.

"Where are you bleeding from?" She's pulled out her phone.

I stumble forward, reach for the door handle to support myself.

"Stay here. You need help!"

"I'll get security," I say. "You call an ambulance, keep an eye on Piers. He's lost it."

Alison jabs at her phone, then raises it to her ear.

"No," Piers manages to get the word out.

But I turn and stumble through to the wings of the *Sharpe* studio, slamming the door behind me.

CHAPTER TWENTY-FIVE

THEY'RE NOT EXPECTING ANYONE to run onstage from the Green Room, that's clear. The security guards are stationed watching the audience. I lean against the wall for a moment to compose myself.

There's my dad, in the chair at the center of the lights. That gray hair, thinning on top. The elegantly trimmed beard that feels so reassuring when he kisses my cheek. He looks older. Exhausted. I wonder when he last slept.

Marcus asks him something, and he rolls up his sleeve, and points to the blue dot on his arm. The tattoo the Home Secretary gave him when he fell asleep after sitting up all night with me, those long nights after Mum and Rebecca were killed.

I try to swallow, but it feels like something's stuck in my throat.

There's laughter, from the audience, but Dad doesn't smile. He rolls his sleeve back down.

I could go back to the Green Room. Get my wound discreetly treated and go home with Dad. Piers will take care of what happened at the hospital, cover up the rest, and everything will be okay. Dad will forgive me. We'll move to Downing Street, and there will be more time together. Dad will make things better. Improve the children's homes, look into special cases, exceptions. I know he'll keep his word on that.

But it isn't enough. And it won't save Tig.

Walking straight is tough. In fact, walking at all takes a lot of energy. I want to stop, to lie down on the cool tile floor. Instead I push myself, and I reel slowly into the studio itself.

People react as I come into view, under the blaze of the lights. The man with the clipboard hisses something at me, and waves back toward the Green Room. But I have momentum now, and I stumble further onto the stage. He reaches for my arm, but I shove my phone into his outstretched hand.

"There's video on here you need to see."

Then I stumble on. To my Dad.

The audience sees me. There's a sound from them, like a wave of whispers. I concentrate on my walk. One foot in front of the other. Try to stay straight. I probably look like I'm drunk.

Now Dad notices me. He stops mid-gesture. He was spreading his hands wide, but now he looks as if he's been left holding an invisible box. For a moment I want to laugh. I'm lightheaded. That can't be good.

He jumps to his feet. "Talia. What are you doing?"

The two security guards turn and head for me. But Marcus Sharpe holds up a hand, halting them.

"Miss Hale," he says, eyes wide. "We weren't expecting you."

Dad steps up protectively, moving between me and the cameras.

"My daughter isn't well. Can we please take a break while I look after her?"

Marcus stands. "Perhaps now would be a good time to cut to —"

"Dad, you have to help her. She'll die if you don't."

There's a pause, an audible intake of breath of the crowd. I feel as if they've pulled away from me, the sea pulling away from the shore, before coming back as a tsunami of muttering.

Marcus speaks. "Who'll die?"

"No one," Dad says too quickly. He puts a gentle hand on my shoulder.

"As you all know, Talia has been ill. She's feverish. Hallucinating. It's best if we take a quick break for commercial now and come back once we've got her some help."

Wow. That was cold.

I pull away from my father. But he doesn't look angry. There's worry in his eyes. Perhaps he really thinks I am delusional. It would make sense to him. Explain why I'd run away. Why I'd gone to the Barbican. Why his good girl had gone so far off the rails.

This is my last chance. I can play along, pretend I am feverish. I'm sure a court would buy it, would let me off with another slap on the wrist. I can go home. And Dad's right, he's not in power yet. Won't be in time to save Tig. So what's the point in throwing my life away? There's nothing Dad can do.

Then it hits me. There is one thing Dad could do.

He could lose.

If Sebastian Conway won, he'd stop this madness.

Deep breath. I break eye contact. Can I do this to Dad?

"I'm fine." That's not true. It's hard to talk. Hard to focus. "And I have some questions for my father."

Out of the corner of my eye I see Marcus give a little shake of his head to someone off-screen, then gestures for a microphone. We're staying live. He knows this could be scandalous, could raise the ratings. This could save his career.

"I'm not sick anymore. And I'm certainly not deluded."

Dad seems far away, like he's at the other end of a tunnel. I want to reach for him. But I glance at the lights on the cameras instead, still green. Still broadcasting.

Marcus steps forward, microphone pointed at me. I take it from his hand.

One last game of Interview with my father.

"Dad started this for my mother and my sister, and to prevent other families losing loved ones." I sway a little. "Then he lost sight of that."

I look up into Dad's wide eyes and feel like I've stabbed him. He looks so betrayed. I don't want to twist the knife. I just want to go home. With him.

"Some—." I pause, swallow down a sob. "Somewhere along the line it became about revenge on criminals. There's a girl dying in the Barbican. The girl from the hospital. She's my sister's age and he won't save her. So my question is: When did politics become more important than children's lives?"

I hold the mic out to him. His arm is across his stomach, as if he's been punched. I want to take it all back.

The crowd is silent.

"I ... nothing is more important than children's lives, but ..."

He tails off. He's usually so good at this.

"I'm sorry Dad. I really am." It comes out as a whisper.

Only his chest is moving. I watch it as he breathes. In. Out. In. Out. His eyes glisten.

He glances up at the camera. "Can we cut away? This is a private matter, and —"

His words are distorting in my ears. I'm ripping his dream from him. Losing the only family I have left. But I keep talking.

"It's not private. Tig is dying. But you won't do anything. Why?"

Dad's mouth opens and closes. But then he straightens up. Becomes the politician I've seen on television.

"I don't personally know what conditions are like in the Barbican, but the people who built the barricades are clearly to blame for any fatalities and ..."

The audience are on their feet, some cheering, some booing, all shouting.

"But my party and I have always stood for justice."

I've lost him. The room is spinning now.

"My daughter has been through a traumatic few weeks and I think she should be in bed."

The sound rises and falls, like waves in my ears. I reach out for something to support myself.

There's nothing to hold on to. I tip toward the ground. Dad catches me, just in time, clutching my injured arm. I scream as he crushes my wound. The warm blood saturates the arm of my jumper again, flowing fast. It's running down my fingers now, dribbling onto the floor. Dad stares at me in confusion. He pulls his hand away and looks at it, obviously surprised to see the red. Released from his grasp, I start to fall.

"No! Talia!"

It feels so slow. The studio lights are like a carnival, spinning and blurring as I tumble backwards. Marcus Sharpe's carefully shaped brows furrow. The mouths of the audience members are open, some still shouting or cheering, some with the wide "oh" of shock at the blood, at the falling girl.

Dad reaches for me too late. His mouth is still moving but I can't make out the words. It's like the howling of a dog. Maybe he's screaming. Maybe he's yelling at me.

He should. I've betrayed him. My head thumps against the floor, hard, but there's no pain.

Darkness comes, warm as a blanket.

CHAPTER TWENTY-SIX

I WAKE SLOWLY, AS if I'm pulling myself up from a great depth. It doesn't occur to me to be surprised that I wake at all. There's pain; a distant ache, like it's hovering above me, waiting to land.

Something beeps at my side, and there's shouting not far away. That's what woke me up. A unit sits next to my bed with lights on it. That's where the beeping's coming from.

It looks like a Transfer machine.

Of course. I stole the antibiotics, broke out of the Barbican, ran from the police. I briefly wonder what I've been sentenced to. But the pain is different. An ache, not the sharp pressure of the disease being forced into my blood and body. And there's a line on the machine, bobbing up and down.

It's not a Transfer machine, then. It's familiar. I remember being hooked up to one of these after Rebecca and Mum were murdered. This is a heart monitor.

The shouting starts again and I crane my neck to see where it's coming from.

There are two blurred figures framed in a white doorway. One is trying to push through.

"I'm her friend, okay? Back off and let me in."

I know that voice.

"Galen?" My voice is weak, as if I haven't used it in a long time. But both the figures freeze and turn to me.

"She's awake!" Galen pushes past the other man, who's wearing some kind of black uniform. Security, I guess. Galen is at my side in seconds.

The security guard hovers in the doorway.

"Get a nurse! Now!" Galen says, and the guard disappears.

I can focus a little better now, on the green of those startling eyes. I raise my hand to my head, and there's a sharp jab of pain in my hand. I peer down. A tube sticks out of the back of my hand. An IV feeds into it.

"Are you okay?" Galen asks, then shakes his head. "Stupid question. Of course not. Can you talk?"

I try. My tongue feels thick in my mouth, too slow, too big.

"Hi," I say to test myself. My voice slurs slightly, but it's intelligible. "What happened?"

"You collapsed. On live TV. You got shot."

My arm aches where I took the bullet. I remember that clearly enough. But why does my head hurt so much?

"Where am I?" I know it's a cliché to ask.

"St. Thomas's Hospital."

No Transfer center here, only an accident and injuries unit. I peer around at the flowers on the side table, the cards on the chest of drawers. There are a lot of them.

I remember snatches of the last few days. I shuffle them in my mind, trying to make sense out of them. I remember betraying Dad. Then it hits me. The reason I did it.

I sit up and grab Galen's arm, almost ripping out the IV. "How's Tig?"

He smiles, and it's a big smile, lighting his face. "Recovering well, thanks to you. Right after the interview, the Government agreed to allow safe passage to paramedics. They were desperate for votes and saw an opportunity after what you said. Wanted to appear compassionate. Tig got taken straight to hospital."

I fall back onto the pillows, dizzy with relief. Tig is okay. I think of her thin little fox face. Of her smiling when I made her honey and lemon.

"She's still weak, but the x-rays show her lungs are clearing, slowly. She's been asking about you. I'll bring her here as soon as you're both well enough."

"I'd like that." I close my eyes and breathe deeply. I'm not sure I want to know the answer to the next question. "And the election? Who's winning? What do the polls say?"

"It's over. Sebastian Conway won. Your appearance on *Sharpe* made headline news, along with that footage you shot. It swung it just enough."

I swallow down the tears that threaten to come. Dad lost. Because of me. No wonder he isn't here. I wonder if I'll ever see him again. What I'm going to do.

But it was worth it, if Tig's recovering.

"The Barbican?"

"Repairing itself. The martial law Transfers have been stopped and the Recall ended. You even impressed the lads. No one's taken a bullet for us before."

I glance at the bandage on my arm. "Oh, this old thing?" I shrug. "I've had worse."

Galen laughs at that. He's standing right next to me now, looking down at me as if I'm the most amazing thing on earth, and my cheeks warm. "Thank you," he says, in a whisper. "There's a real chance things can change now."

"No ... no problem," I stutter. "All I did was fix the stuff I screwed up. Most of it was my fault in the first place. I made a lot of mistakes."

I'm babbling. But I can't seem to stop. "I'm sorry. I got everything wrong."

"Yeah." He gives a little laugh. "But that's what makes you brilliant. Do you know how few people can admit that? Never mind go all out to fix it."

He pushes my hair out of my face. Then he's leaning in. He pauses for a moment, as if waiting for permission. His breath is soft on my mouth, green eyes so close to mine. I smile, and then he's kissing me, so carefully. His lips are barely touching mine, soft and gentle, and I push myself up from the pillow into the kiss. He slides a hand behind my head and cradles it. The throbbing in my head recedes, and once again there is nothing but him, the stubble of his face brushing against my cheek, the smell of him, the warmth of him.

Then there's a cough.

It's a nurse, standing in the room behind Galen. He pulls away, and she approaches, eyebrow raised.

"Sorry to interrupt. Good to see you're awake." She checks the machines and my pulse. I notice the beeping is a little more rapid since Galen kissed me. The nurse puts on a blood pressure cuff and peers into my eyes. When she's finally done, she nods and smiles.

"Everything looks good, but the doctor will be in as soon as he can to make sure. I'll let your dad know," she says, then disappears out through the door.

I'm lucky. I know it. How many people can say they got shot twice and survived?

Another thought filters through my addled brain.

"Wait. Did that nurse say she'd let my father know?"

Galen nods. "He's been here almost the whole time. Even during the election results. He sent a written concession speech. Wouldn't let me in, of course. I had to wait until he popped out to try to get to see you."

I'm not sure how I feel. What does that mean? I thought Dad would have given up on me. I destroyed his dreams. Maybe he has.

Maybe he needed to tell me in person how badly I betrayed his trust.

But he's been here the whole time? How long is the whole time? I look to the window. Gray buildings block most of the view, but the shadows are long, and lights are on in a few offices. Early evening, then, but what day?

"How long have I been unconscious?"

"Three days. You hit your head hard on the studio floor. You had blood transfusions, and an operation on the gunshot wound, but it was the head injury that kept you unconscious."

That explains the ache in my head, then. But another question filters through my foggy mind.

"Why am I not in Quarantine? Am I under arrest?"

Galen shakes his head. "Sebastian Conway's given his word — nonviolent crimes committed during the blockade won't be prosecuted. That includes you."

I breathe deeply. It's more than I dared to hope. I won't have to go through the torture of the Transfer again.

"But what's going to happen to Tig? Will she be sentenced and returned to the home?"

"The new Government put a freeze on Transfers to children. But she will have to go back to the home. I'm going to apply to be her legal guardian. They're talking about changing the laws on treating the sick, on prosecuting doctors. There might be an amnesty for us."

There's sadness in his eyes as he says it.

"But it's too late for your dad."

Galen's Adam's apple bobs. "Yeah, but there's hope. His legal aid lawyer says he's not fit to stand trial. He might get hospital instead of prison." He strokes my forehead again. "Thank you. His lawyer said you asked for a doctor to examine him."

I forgot I asked Frank for that, but I'm glad he lived up to his word. I doubt they can fix the brain damage. But they can deal with him compassionately, at least.

Galen continues. "There's still so much to be done, and we need your help. Even after everything, almost half the country voted against Sebastian Conway. They saw your videos. Saw families and old people being dragged from their homes, and voted for more of the same."

"How can I stop that?"

"We need a spokesperson. People trust you. The media are clamoring for interviews. You can tell them what it's really like for us. Tell people why they should care."

I laugh. "You don't need other people speaking for you. That's what got us into this mess. Only you can tell them what it's really like. But I can help make them listen."

Galen picks up my hand and squeezes it.

And that's when Dad walks in.

"Talia? Talia!" He rushes to my side. Galen drops my hand, and steps back.

"They called to say you'd woken. I got here as soon as I could." He's shaking. There are dark bags under his eyes. "How are you?"

"Woozy. Awake." I lie there, and stare at him. "I didn't think you'd be here."

"I'm sorry I wasn't here when you woke. I had to give a proper concession speech, and tender my resignation to the party."

"Did ... did they make you do that?"

Dad's eyes look hollow. "Not yet. But they would have. It was better for everyone that I did it without being forced."

I'm not sure what to say. "I'm sorry. But I had to save Tig."

"Maybe I deserved what you did. At least a little. I got caught up in politics. I regret the way I treated you at the studio. I might have lost sight of things. I didn't realize until I almost lost you." He gives an odd laugh. "Compared to that, losing the election wasn't so bad."

He picks up my hand, holds it between his warm palms. "Will you come home when this is done? Try to fix things between us?"

I stare at his neat fingernails, feeling the longing for home. Fighting the urge to agree at once.

"I'm going to keep working to improve life for everyone in the Barbican," I say. "Would you still want me around doing that?"

Dad pauses for a long time. "That's your decision. You're nearly an adult."

"Will Alison be around?"

"Yes. In fact, I want her to move in."

She wasn't only interested in being the prime minister's wife, then. Maybe I've made some mistakes myself. Maybe I've got her wrong. She was nice to me when I was sick, and she saved me from Piers. But it won't be just Dad and me in the flat anymore.

An idea occurs to me.

"I'll move back home on one condition," I say. "And it'll require you and Galen to agree."

Galen snaps his head around. "Me?"

"Yes. To my father fostering Tig so she doesn't have to go back to the home. Only until you become Tig's legal guardian."

My father opens his mouth, but I'm not finished. I turn to him.

"And Galen can come and visit her any time he likes."

That's struck my father silent. Galen is quiet too, staring at Dad from across the bed. He must know this is the best thing for his sister. But I doubt he likes the idea.

"You'd be there, Talia?" Galen says. "Looking after Tig?"

"Of course, when she's not at school. Along with Dad, Alison, and you."

A deep breath. "Then I guess it's okay. For my sister's sake."

"Dad?"

My father is staring at Galen, and I can almost read his mind. He'd have to let this criminal into his home. He'd have to trust him not to hurt us like Thomas Bryce did.

I wonder if Dad can do that.

"She's Rebecca's age, Dad. And the homes are awful."

It's a long time before he answers. "Okay. But only for the girl's sake, and yours, Talia."

I lean back on my pillows. My heart flips at the idea of Galen's visits. And our beautiful flat wouldn't seem hollow anymore, filled with Tig's laughter.

"Shake on it," I say.

"What?" Galen asks.

"You heard me."

Dad and Galen look at each other. To my surprise, it's Dad who reaches out first, across my bed. Galen hesitates, then puts his arm out, and his palm hits Dad's. A little too hard. But they shake. I stare at their interlocked hands.

It'll take a lot to make this work, but they'll come to respect each other.

Probably.

Galen was right. There's so much to be done — in the Barbican and everywhere else. I have to get people to listen, to open their minds. To change.

But if I can get my father and Galen to shake hands, I can do anything.

ACKNOWLEDGEMENTS

So many people helped me at different times, and I'm sure I've forgotten some people I should be thanking. So I'll start off by apologizing to them. Sorry. I should have kept a proper list all along, but I wasn't sure this day would come.

Special thanks to the following people.

Barry Jowett & the amazing team at DCB/Cormorant for making this book real, for their enthusiasm, editing, a wonderful cover, promotion, all of it. It's a lot of work to get a book out, and I really appreciate them taking a chance on my story.

My teachers. Especially Ibi Kaslik, Elizabeth Ruth, Rob Weston and Anne Lauren Carter.

My fellow Kidcritters for the constant support, advice and crits. You made rewriting fun, and improved this book immeasurably. Particular thanks to Valerie Sherrard. This book would not be here without your help.

The wonderful Beta readers of my writing: Pier Van Tijn, Lena Coakley, Jo Hope, Tanis Rideout and my Mum for their time and helpful feedback.

Rebecca Swift and The Literary Consultancy in the UK, who

championed my writing by featuring me in their showcase, trying to get me an agent, and short-listing me for their Pen Factor competition. They also gave me great feedback on my work.

CANSCAIP, who have been a great source of inspiration, particularly the Packaging Your Imagination conference each year. Jacqueline Guest gave me excellent advice and plenty of encouragement in her role as the CANSCAIP Writer in Residence. The monthly meetings have been a lovely opportunity to mingle with authors and emerging writers. Seeing other people get published around me made it all seem possible.

The Blairs — my wonderful in-laws, for their kindness and support in everything.

My mum, who encouraged my writing from a very early age, and my father and my sister, who were all subjected to countless drafts of my work long before I had anything readable. Jo, Mum and Dad, I am sorry for all the terrible writing I put you through.

My final thanks must go to my fantastic husband, Matt. Without his help, I'd have no time to write, or wonderful children to distract me from it.